ONCE IN A LIFETIME

A COMEDY IN THREE ACTS

BY

MOSS HART AND GEORGE S. KAUFMAN

SAMUEL FRENCH, INC.
45 WEST 25TH STREET   NEW YORK 10010
7623 SUNSET BOULEVARD   HOLLYWOOD 90046
LONDON   *TORONTO*

The following is a copy of program of the first performance of "ONCE IN A LIFETIME," as produced at the Music Box, New York City:

SAM H. HARRIS

Presents

"ONCE IN A LIFETIME"

A Comedy In Three Acts

By MOSS HART *and* GEORGE S. KAUFMAN

Staged by George S. Kaufman

GEORGE LEWIS	*Hugh O'Connell*
MARY DANIELS	*Jean Dixon*
JERRY HYLAND	*Grant Mills*
THE PORTER	*Oscar Polk*
HELEN HOBART	*Spring Byington*
SUSAN WALKER	*Sally Phipps*
CIGARETTE GIRL	*Clara Waring*
COAT CHECK GIRL	*Otis Schaefer*
PHYLLIS FONTAINE	*Janet Currie*
MISS FONTAINE'S MAID	*Marie Ferguson*
MISS FONTAINE'S CHAUFFEUR	*Charles Mack*
FLORABEL LEIGH	*Eugenie Frontai*
MISS LEIGH'S MAID	*Dorothy Talbot*
MISS LEIGH'S CHAUFFEUR	*Edward Loud*
BELLBOY	*Payson Crane*
MRS. WALKER	*Frances E. Brandt*
ERNEST	*Marc Leobell*
HERMAN GLOGAUER	*Charles Halton*
MISS LEIGHTON	*Leona Maricle*
LAWRENCE VAIL	*George S. Kaufman*
WEISSKOPF	*Louis Cruger*
METERSTEIN	*William McFadden*
FIRST PAGE	*Stanley Fitzpatrick*
SECOND PAGE	*Edwin Mills*
THREE SCENARIO WRITERS—*Kempton Race, George Casselbury and Burton Mallory*	
RUDOLPH KAMMERLING	*Walter Dreher*
FIRST ELECTRICIAN	*Jack Williams*
SECOND ELECTRICIAN	*John O. Hewitt*
A VOICE PUPIL	*Jane Buchanan*
MR. FLICK	*Harold Grau*

ORIGINAL PROGRAM—*Continued*

MISS CHASEN .... *Virginia Hawkins*
FIRST CAMERAMAN .... *Irving Morrow*
THE BISHOP .... *Granville Bates*
THE SIXTH BRIDESMAID .... *Frances Thress*
SCRIPT GIRL .... *Georgia MacKinnon*
GEORGE'S SECRETARY .... *Robert Ryder*

THE SCENES

ACT I. SCENE I. *A room in the West Forties, New York.*
SCENE II. *A Pullman Car.*
SCENE III. *The Gold Room of the Hotel Stilton, Los Angeles.*

ACT II. *Reception Room of the Glogauer Studio.*

ACT III. SCENE I. *On the set.*
SCENE II. *The Pullman Car.*
SCENE III. *The Reception Room.*

DESCRIPTION OF CHARACTERS

GEORGE: *A magnetic, fair-haired young vaudeville actor. Good-natured and inclined toward stoutness. Age 30.*

MAY: *A wholesome, common-sense, substantial vaudeville actress. Dry sense of humor. Age 25.*

JERRY: *Tall, slender and good-looking. Age 32.*

PORTER: *Colored man.*

HELEN: *Plump, aggressive, talkative, good-looking. Age 35.*

SUSAN: *A typical pretty, small city girl.*

PHYLLIS and FLORABEL: *Two contrasting types of movie stars.*

MRS. WALKER: *Well dressed; ambitious for her daughter. Aged 45-50.*

GLOGAUER: *A good-natured, nervous, energetic little Jewish picture magnate. Aged 50.*

MISS LEIGHTON: *Is pretty, much like the furniture of the studio. She wears a flowing black evening gown, although it is early morning, fondles a long string of pearls, and behaves very much like Elinor Glyn.*

LAWRENCE VAIL: *A slim, black-haired young man.*

KAMMERLING: *A big, brusque, excitable German. Aged 40.*

BISHOP. *A stout, benevolent-looking man of 55.*

Other characters to be of variegated types.

Once In A Lifetime

ACT ONE

SCENE I

SCENE: *The scene is a furnished room in the West Forties, New York. The wall Right rakes toward Center, with a door down R. In the back wall, R.C., there is a window. At a jog in the back flat L.C. there is a washbowl. There is a double bed in the corner up R., and a Morris chair down L.C. with a table beside it on which is a reading lamp. There is a tabloid newspaper on the bed, and a "Saturday Evening Post" and a box of Indian nuts on the table.*

At the rise, GEORGE LEWIS is discovered deep in the Morris chair, immersed to the exclusion of all else in a copy of "Variety." He has a box of Indian nuts beside him, and these he proceeds to crack and eat with a methodical thoroughness. After two have been cracked, there is a knock at the door.

GEORGE. Come in!
MAY DANIELS. *(Enters R.)* Hello, George.
GEORGE. Hello.
MAY. Jerry not back yet, huh?
GEORGE. No.

7

MAY. Anything new since this afternoon? You haven't heard anything, have you? *(She sits on bed.)*

GEORGE. No. Are you going to stay and talk, May? I'm reading.

MAY. What time's Jerry coming back, do you know?

GEORGE. *(Shakes his head)* He went to a show.

MAY. It's wonderful how you two take it. You off to ball games every day, Jerry going to shows! What about the old vaudeville act? Are we gonna get some bookings or aren't we?

GEORGE. I don't know anything about it, May. I'm reading.

MAY. Still *"Variety"?*

GEORGE. Uh-huh.

MAY. One of these days you'll pick up a paper that's written in English—and you'll have to send out for an interpreter.

GEORGE. What do you mean? *"Variety"* is in English.

MAY. All right.

GEORGE. It has news of the show world from different countries, but it's all in English.

MAY. *(Rising, crossing c.)* I said all right, George.

GEORGE. Want some Indian nuts?

MAY. No, thanks. *(Watches him as he goes back to the nuts)* Don't your teeth ever bother you?

GEORGE. No. Why?

MAY. I dunno—after all those damn things you've eaten. Do you realize, George, that you've left a trail of Indian nuts clean across the United States? If you ever commit a crime they could go right *to* you.

GEORGE. *(Going back to his reading)* Aw!

MAY. You've thrown them shells under radiators in every dollar-and-a-half hotel from here to Seattle. I can visualize hundreds of chambermaids, the country over, coming in the morning you check out and murmuring a blessing on your head. Don't you ever have bad dreams, George, with that on your mind?

GEORGE. Listen, May, are you gonna keep talking till Jerry gets here?

MAY. *(Pacing R. and L.)* What's Jerry up to, George? Is he going to land us something, or isn'i he? How much longer are we going to lay around here?

GEORGE. Don't ask me—ask Jerry.

MAY. *(Still pacing up and down R.)* I'm gonna. And we'll have a showdown tonight. The Automat don't spell home to me.

GEORGE. We don't live there.

MAY. We do everything but sleep there, and we'd be doing that if they could get beds into them slots.

GEORGE. You oughta have patience, May. We've only been here four weeks.

MAY. George, listen. Dumb as you are, you ought to be able to get this: The bankbook says there's just one hundred and twenty-eight dollars left. One hundred and twenty-eight dollars. Get that?

GEORGE. Sure.

MAY. Well, how long do you think three people can live on that, with Jerry going to opening nights and you taking in the World Series?

GEORGE. Something'll turn up. It always does. *(He cracks a nut.)*

MAY. *(At window; turns)* Well, I'm glad you like those goddam things—you're certainly a lucky fellow. Because the way things are going you may have to live on 'em in another week.

GEORGE. Go on, May—nobody could live on Indian nuts. There isn't enough to 'em. Look—that's all they are. *(Showing her as he eats one.)*

MAY. All right, George. *(A moment's restless pacing)* Well, I suppose it's another week of hang-

ing around offices, and another series of those nickel-
plated dinners. I'm so sick of the whole business I
could yell.

GEORGE. You're just blue, May.

MAY. I wouldn't wonder. Living alone in that
hall bedroom—without even the crack of an Indian
nut to cheer you up. Well! I wanted to do it, and
here I am. I guess it's better than selling ninety-
cent perfume to the feminine population of Connels-
ville, Pa., but there's times when I wish I was back
there.

GEORGE. Maybe we'll play there some day.

MAY. It wouldn't surprise me.

GEORGE. I wonder if we'll ever play Medallion—
I haven't been back for four years.

MAY. Has it got an Automat?

GEORGE. I don't think so.

MAY. *(Sits on bed)* We'll never play it.

GEORGE. Jerry did play it once—that's where he
discovered me. He played the theatre I was working in—I was an usher.

MAY. Yah, I remember. Too bad that was pre-
Roxy, George—you'd have had a career.

GEORGE. If I'd have stayed I might have been a
lieutenant. One of the boys I started with is a
major.

MAY. Do you think they'll ever have conscrip-
tion for theatre ushers?

GEORGE. Then Jerry came along and he offered
me this job. He said I was just right for it.

MAY. He had a good eye. As far as I'm concerned you're the best dead-pan feeder in all show
business.

GEORGE. Don't the audiences like me too?

MAY. No one ever gave birth in the aisle, George.
but you're all right.

GEORGE. I love doing it, too. The longer we play
the act the more I like it.

MAY. George, you and Jerry have been bunking together for four years. Isn't Jerry a swell guy?

GEORGE. He's been a wonderful friend to me.

MAY. *(Looking at him)* I wouldn't tell this to him, George, but I'll never forget what I owe Jerry Hyland. *(Quickly)* And don't you go telling him, either.

GEORGE. I won't tell him. How much do you owe him?

MAY. George, please stop eating those things— they're going to your head. I don't mean I owe him any money. But he's never made me feel that we were anything but good friends, or that I'd have to feel anyways else to keep the job.

GEORGE. He never made me feel anything, either.

MAY. Well, that's just dandy.

GEORGE. Shall I tell you something, May?

MAY. I wish you would.

GEORGE. I think Jerry likes you.

MAY. All right, George.

GEORGE. No—I mean he *really* likes you—a whole lot.

MAY. *(Rises)* O. K., George. The question is: What do we do about bookings? Are we going to crash the big time or aren't we?

GEORGE. We were doing all right on the small time. We could be working right along—you know what the Booking Office told us.

MAY. And you know where the Booking Office books us. Bellows Falls, Vermont.

GEORGE. I liked it there.

MAY. What?

GEORGE. We had a good dinner there. With jello. *(Cracks nut.)*

MAY. Look, George. Don't you want to do anything else all your life but knock about all over the map as a small-time vaudeville actor?

GEORGE. No.

MAY. You don't?

GEORGE. No.

MAY. Well, I guess that settles that, doesn't it? You might as well go ahead and read.

GEORGE. No, I feel like talking now.

MAY. I feel like reading now. (JERRY HYLAND *enters* R.) Well, here we are. When do we play the Palace?

GEORGE. Hello, Jerry.

MAY. Or did you settle for the last half in Bridgeport?

JERRY. May, it's here!

MAY. You got bookings?

GEORGE. Is it the Palace?

JERRY. (*Crosses to table; throws hat down*) Never mind about that. I've got some news for you. I saw history made tonight!

MAY. What are you talking about?

GEORGE. (*Simultaneously with* MAY) You **saw** what?

JERRY. I've just been to the opening of Al Jolson's talking picture, "The Jazz Singer."

MAY. Well, what of it?

JERRY. And I'm telling you it's the greatest thing in the world.

MAY. There've been good pictures before, Jerry.

JERRY. I'm not talking about the picture. I mean the Vitaphone.

MAY. The what?

JERRY. The Vitaphone—the talkies.

GEORGE. They talk.

MAY. Oh, that!

JERRY. That! You ought to hear them cheering, May! Everybody went nuts! I tell you, May, it's going to revolutionize the entire industry. It's something so big I bet even the Vitaphone people don't know what they've got yet. You've got to hear it, May, to realize what it means.

MAY. Come out of it, Jerry——

JERRY. *(Continuing)* Why, in six months from now——

MAY. *(Continuing)* What are *you* getting so het up about? It's no money in your pocket even if it is good.

(Together)

GEORGE. No.

JERRY. No? *(A pause)* Well, we're leaving for Los Angeles in the morning.

MAY. What did you say?

JERRY. We're leaving for Los Angeles in the morning.

GEORGE. What time?

MAY. Are you out of your mind?

JERRY. *(Just about as fast as he can talk)* Don't you understand, May? For the next six months they won't know which way to turn. All the old standbys are going to find themselves out in the cold, and somebody with brains and sense enough to use them is going to get into the big dough. The movies are back where they were when the De Milles and the Laskys first saw what they were going to amount to! Can't you see what it would mean to get in *now?*

MAY. What do you mean, get in, Jerry? What would *we* do there—act, or what?

JERRY. No, no! Acting is small potatoes from now on. You can't tell what we'll do—direct, give orders, tell 'em how to do things! There's no limit to where we can go!

MAY. *(Vaguely groping)* Yah, but what do we know about——

JERRY. Good Lord, May! We've been doing nothing but playing the act in all the small-time houses in the country. Suppose we *do* cut loose and go out there? What have we got to lose?

GEORGE. A hundred and twenty-eight dollars. *(Cracks nut.)*

MAY. Shut up, George! I don't know, Jerry——

JERRY. We gotta get out there, May! Before this Broadway bunch climbs on the bandwagon. There's going to be a gold rush, May. There's going to be a trek out to Hollywood that'll make the Forty-niners look sick.

MAY. Y'mean thar's gold in them hills, Jerry?

JERRY. *(He has hardly paused for breath)* Gold and a black marble swimming pool, with the Jap chauffeur waiting outside the iron-grilled gate—all that and more, May, if we can work it right and get in *now*. They're panicstricken out there. They'll fall on the neck of the first guy that seems to know what it's all about. And that's why we gotta get there quick.

MAY. Yah, but give me time to think, Jerry. *(Sits on bed)* Suppose we don't catch on right away—how are we going to live? You heard what the boy wonder said—a hundred and twenty-eight dollars.

JERRY. *(A moment's pause)* I've got five hundred more.

MAY. *(Rises)* What!

JERRY. I've got five hundred more. Right here.

MAY. Where'd you get it?

JERRY. Now don't yell, May. I sold our act.

MAY. What?

JERRY. I sold the act! I took one look at that picture and sold the act outright to Eddie Garvey and the Sherman Sisters for five hundred cash. Now don't get sore, May. It was the only thing to do.

MAY. *(Slowly)* No. I'm not getting sore, Jerry, but——

GEORGE. *(Coming to life)* You sold the act to the Sherman sisters?

JERRY. *(Again the sales talk)* My God, if people once took a mule and a covered wagon just because they heard of some mud that looked yellow, and en-

dured hardships and went all the way across the
country with their families—fought Indians, even—
think what it'll mean, May, if we win out! No more
traveling all over the country—living in one place,
instead of——

MAY. Okay, Jerry—I'm with you. You had some
helluva nerve, but count me in.

JERRY. Good for you! How about you, George?

GEORGE. What?

JERRY. Are you willing to take a chance with us
—leave all this behind and cut loose for Hollywood?

GEORGE. Well, but look—if you sold the act——

JERRY. Sure I sold the act. We're going out and
try this new game. Now what do you say?

MAY. Come on, George!

JERRY. It's the chance of a life-   *(Together)*
time!

GEORGE. But what'll we do there?

JERRY. We can talk that over on the train. The
important thing is to get out there and to get there
fast!

GEORGE. But if you've sold the act——

JERRY. Oh! *(A turn upstage.)*

MAY. George, listen. We're giving up the act.
We're not going to do the act any more. Don't you
understand that?

GEORGE. Yah, but he sold the act——

MAY. I *understand* that he sold the act. Look,
George. *(As to a small child)* There is a new in-
vention called talking pictures. In these pictures
the actors will not only be seen but will also talk.
For the first time in the history of pictures they
will use their voices. *(She pauses; resumes in an
altered tone)* I've got an idea.

JERRY. What?

MAY. I think I know what we're going to do out
there.

JERRY. Well!?

MAY. Most of these bozoes haven't ever talked on a stage. They've never spoken lines before.

JERRY. They gotta learn, that's all.

MAY. Yah. You bet they do. And who's going to teach them? *(Her eye travels to the two of them)* We'll open a school of elocution and voice culture.

JERRY. What?

MAY. We'll open a school, Jerry—teach 'em how to talk. They're sure to fall for it, because they'll be scared stiff. We'll have them coming to us instead of our going to them.

JERRY. Yah, but—but us with a school, May. We don't know anything about it.

MAY. Maybe *you* don't, but *I* went to one once. And it's easy.

JERRY. But what do you have to do? Can I learn it?   *(Warn BLACKOUT and CURTAIN.)*

MAY. Sure! Anyhow, I'll do all that.

GEORGE. *What* are you going to do?⎰ *(Together)*
MAY. I tell you it's natural, Jerry.⎱

JERRY. *(Quieting* BOTH *of them)* Shut up a minute, will you? Let me think. Maybe you got hold of something! A school of elocution. It might not be a bad idea.

GEORGE. What's elocution?

MAY. It's a swell idea. And if I know actors, Jerry, they'll come running. Why, between you and I and the lamp-post here—*(She takes in* GEORGE*)* —it's the best idea anybody ever had. How soon we gonna leave?

JERRY. Tomorrow! As soon as you see the picture. I want you to see the picture first.

MAY. O. K. Twenty-five of that five hundred goes for books on elocution first thing in the morning. I'll learn this racket or know the reason why.

GEORGE. *(Rises)* But what'll *I* do? I don't know anything about elocution.

MAY. George, you don't know anything about anything, and if what they say about the movies is true, you'll go far. *(Swinging to* JERRY*)* So help me, Jerry, it'll work out like a charm—you watch if it doesn't! It's coming back to me already—I remember Lesson Number One. *(Paces down* L.*)*

JERRY. Well, if you're sure you can get away with it, May——

MAY. It's a cinch! Just watch! Come here, George! I'll try it on George! *(She is* L. *of* GEORGE. JERRY *is on his* R.*)*

GEORGE. What?

MAY. Say "California, here I come."

GEORGE. Why should I?

MAY. Don't argue—say it!

GEORGE. "California, here I come."

MAY. Now, then—stomach in, chest out. Wait a minute—maybe it's the other way around. No, that's right—stomach in, chest out. Now say it again.

GEORGE. *(Better this time)* "California, here I come."

MAY. Now this time with feeling. You are about to start on a great adventure—the covered wagon is slowly moving across the plains to a marble swimming pool! Let's have it, George—give it everything!

GEORGE. *(With feeling)* "California, here I come."

JERRY. Yay!

MAY. Yay! It works, Jerry—it works! } *(Together)*

JERRY. And if it works on George it'll work on anybody!

MAY. California, here we come!

BLACKOUT

ACT ONE

SCENE II

The scene is a corner of a Pullman car, en route to Los Angeles.

At the rise MAY, JERRY *and* GEORGE *are discovered.* MAY *is looking straight out, a troubled expression in her eyes.* JERRY *is doing his two or three hundredth cross word puzzle, and* GEORGE *is eating nuts and reading "Variety," as usual. There is a silence, broken only by the cracking of shells.*

Two sections of the Pullman are shown. JERRY *is seated on the Left seat of the Left section,* MAY *on the Right seat, and* GEORGE *on the Left seat of the Right section, his back to the* OTHERS.

As the Curtain rises, the WHISTLE of the train is heard. GEORGE *cracks an Indian nut.*

MAY. This dust is about an inch thick on me. *(Pause.* GEORGE *cracks another Indian nut.)* George!

GEORGE. Yeah?

MAY. Do those things come without **shells** on them?

GEORGE. I don't think so. Why?

MAY. A few more days of hearing you crack those things and I'll go bugs.

GEORGE. I didn't know they were bothering you, May.

MAY. I was keeping it secret. *(Opens the book on her lap. Reads with venom)* "To teachers of the culture of the human voice——"

JERRY. What's a four-letter word for actor?

MAY. Dope. *(Reading again)* "We strongly urge the use of abdominal breathing as a fundamental principle in elocutionary training." *(The* PORTER *enters* L.*)* "This is a very simple operation and the following methods may be used."

PORTER. You ready to have your berth made up?

MAY. No.

PORTER. Yes, ma'am. *(Starts to go* L.*)*

MAY. All you people know is make up berths. The minute it gets dark you want to make up berths.

PORTER. Lots of times folks want 'em made up.

MAY. Where are we now—pretty near out of this desert?

PORTER. No'm, I guess we're still in it. Pretty dusty, all right.

MAY. It is, huh?

PORTER. Yes, ma'am, it's dusty, all right. Dust all over. See here? *(Runs his hand over arm of seat; shows her.)*

MAY. Thanks.

PORTER. You welcome. *(Nonchalantly wipes his hand off on the pillow he is carrying)* Anything else you want?

MAY. No, that's all, thank you. I just wanted to know if it was dusty.

PORTER. Yes, ma'am, it is.

MAY. I'm ever so much obliged.

PORTER. I guess this your first trip out, ain't it, ma'am?

MAY. How did you know?

PORTER. 'Count of your noticing the dust that way. I've taken out lots of folks—I mean—that was going out for the moving pictures, like you folks— and they always notices the dust.

MAY. They do, huh?

PORTER. Yes, ma'am. But coming back they don't generally care so much. *(Exit L.)*

MAY. Did you hear that? Coming back they don't generally care so much.

JERRY. Oh, come out of it, May. If we don't put up a front like a million dollars, we're lost.

MAY. You know how much of a bankroll we've got, Jerry, and how long it's going to last. And this elocution idea—how do we know it's going to work?

JERRY. It's just around the corner, if we keep our nerve. Think what it'll mean, May, if we put it over.

MAY. Well,—I mustn't go out there this way; it's aging me. But my God, wouldn't you think the railroad would have put a couple of mountains in here somewhere? I'm so sick of looking at wheat and corn—*(A nut cracks)* —and those nuts cracking are beginning to sound like cannons going off.

GEORGE. Why, May——

MAY. *(Rising)* Oh—go ahead and crack two at a time and see if I care. I'm going out to the ladies' smoker. Maybe I'll hear a good dirty story. *(The train WHISTLE is heard. MAY goes out L. There is another heavy silence. GEORGE goes back to his paper and the nuts.)*

JERRY. *(Leaning over back of GEORGE'S seat)* George——

GEORGE. Uh-huh.

JERRY. Listen, you and I have got to pull May out of this. Y'understand?

GEORGE. Sure, but——

JERRY. We've got to keep her spirits up—keep telling her we're going to get away with it.

GEORGE. All right.

JERRY. If she starts anything with you, come right back at her. We can't fall. We're pioneers in

a new field. The talkies are the thing of the future
and there's going to be no stopping them. Got that?

GEORGE. *(Nods. Rises)* The legitimate stage had
better look to its laurels.

JERRY. What?

GEORGE. The legitimate stage had better look to
its laurels. It's in *"Variety."*

JERRY. Sure! That's the idea.

GEORGE. *(Reciting)* "Here is a medium that combines the wide scope of the motion picture with the
finer qualities of the stage proper." It's an inter-
view with Mr. Katzenstein.

JERRY. Let me see it. *(Takes "Variety.")*

GEORGE. *(Wound up)* "It affords opportunities
for entertainment——"

JERRY. All right, all right.

MAY. *(Returns from L.)* Say, what do you think?

GEORGE. What?

MAY. I just saw somebody I know—anyhow, I
used to know her.

JERRY. Who is it?

MAY. This may mean something, Jerry—maybe
the luck's changing.

JERRY. It's Gloria Swanson and she wants to take
lessons.

MAY. Gloria Swanson nothing. It's Helen Hobart.

GEORGE. Helen Hobart! I read her stuff.

MAY. Sure you do, and a million like you. America's foremost movie critic.

GEORGE. And she's on this train.

JERRY. How well do you know her?

MAY. We used to troupe together. I knew her
well enough to tell her she was a rotten actress.

JERRY. What'll we do? Can we get her in here?

MAY. We've got nothing to lose.

JERRY. Ring the bell, George!

GEORGE. *(Pressing buzzer)* Helen Hobart! *(Picks up paper.)*

JERRY. *(Crossing to* R.*)* Say, if she ever sponsored us we'd have all Hollywood begging to get in. She's a powerful important lady, and don't you forget it.

MAY. I don't know whether she'll remember me or not—I didn't dare stop and say hello. The way I feel today I'd break down and cry if anybody ritzed me. (PORTER *enters* L.*)*

JERRY. *(Crossing* L.*)* There's a woman named Miss Helen Hobart in the next car——

MAY. Talking to a young girl. You page her and tell her Miss May Daniels would like to see her.

PORTER. Yes, ma'am.

MAY. And come right back and tell me what she says. *(The* PORTER *goes* L.*)* I'd like to talk to the old battleship again, if only to see her strut her stuff. She's the original iron horse, all right.

JERRY. How long is it since you knew her?

MAY. Plenty. Now listen. If you ever let her know we're just a small-time vaudeville act you'll get the prettiest freeze-out you ever saw. Unless she thinks you're somebody she won't even notice you.

JERRY. Well, what'll we tell her? Let's get together on a story.

MAY. Leave it to me. This is my party.

GEORGE. Don't make up any lies about me.

JERRY. Say, if we could ever get her interested! Her stuff is syndicated all over the country.

GEORGE. It's in two hundred and three newspapers. I was just reading it.

MAY. Yah. It's an awful thought, Jerry, but there must be thousands of guys like George reading that stuff every day.

GEORGE. But it's good.

MAY. And thinking it's good, too. *(Takes paper*

from GEORGE*)* Get this, Jerry. *(Reading)* "Hollywood Happenings, by Helen Hobart. 'Well, movie fans, Wednesday night was just a furore of excitement—the Gold Room at the Stilton just buzzed with the news. But your Helen has managed to get it to you first of all. What do you think? Tina Fair is having her swimming pool done over in eggshell blue.'" How do you like that?

GEORGE. Nice color.

JERRY. They've *all* got swimming pools!

MAY. And if I know Helen she lives and acts just like this column of hers. *(A DOOR CLICKS off* L.*)* Did I hear that door? I did. *(She has taken a quick peep)* Here she comes.

HELEN HOBART. *(Enters* L.*)* My dear! How perfectly lovely! How nice to think of your being on this train.

MAY. Helen, you look marvelous! *(And as a matter of fact,* HELEN *does look little short of marvelous. She literally sparkles with gems. Her ensemble is the Hollywood idea of next year's style a la Metro-Goldwyn.)*

HELEN. Thank you, dear. You haven't changed at all.

MAY. Really? I expected living abroad would change me somewhat.

HELEN. What?

MAY. *(Not stopping)* But let me introduce you to my business manager, Mr. Jerome Hyland——

HELEN. How do you do?

MAY. —and my technical advisor, Doctor Lewis.

HELEN. How do you do, Doctor? (JERRY *murmurs an acknowledgment, but* GEORGE *is too stunned to speak; goes into seat* R.C.*)*

MAY. Please sit down, Helen, and chat awhile. *(They sit.* HELEN *in the* L. *seat of the* L. *section.* MAY R. GEORGE *is hiding in his own seat.* JERRY *is standing* R.*)*

HELEN. Thanks, I will. There's some little girl back in my car who discovered I was Helen Hobart, and she simply won't let me be. That's why I was so glad to get away. She's been reading my column, and she just can't believe I'm human like herself—ha-ha—thinks I'm some sort of goddess. If you *knew* how much of that sort of thing I get.

MAY. *(Innocently)* You're doing some sort of newspaper work, aren't you?

HELEN. *(Amazed—for a full pause)* My dear—didn't you *know?*

MAY. Don't tell me you're a film actress?

HELEN. *(With measured definiteness—from a great height)* I write the most widely syndicated column in the United States. Anybody who reads the newspapers——! But where on earth have you *been,* my dear, that you haven't heard about *me?*

MAY. I've been living in England for the last eight years, Helen. That's probably why I didn't know. But go on and tell me. I'm frightfully interested.

HELEN. Well——! *(She settles herself—after all, this is the thrill that comes once in a lifetime)* If you don't *know,* my dear, I can't quite tell you *all.* But I think I can say in all modesty that I am one of the most important figures in the industry. You know it was I who gave America Gary Cooper, and Rex, the Wonder Horse. Yes, I've done very well for myself. You know I always *could* write, May, but I never expected to be *the* Helen Hobart—ha-ha! (GEORGE *rises; leans, enthralled, over the back of his seat.)* Oh, I can't tell you *everything* one-two-three,—but movie-goers all over the country take my word as law. Of course I earn a perfectly fabulous salary—but I'm hardly allowed to *buy anything* —I'm simply *deluged* with gifts. At Christmas, my dear—well, you'll hardly believe it, but just before

I came East they presented me with a home in Bev-
erly Hills!

MAY. *(In spite of herself)* No kidding!

HELEN. They said I deserved it—that I simply
lived in the studios. I always take an interest in new
pictures in production, you know, and suggest things
to them—and they said that I ought to have a home
I could go to and get away from the studios for a
while. Wasn't that marvelous?

MAY. Marvelous!

HELEN. I call it Parwarmet. I have a penchant
for titles.

MAY. You call it *what?*

HELEN. Parwarmet. You see, I always call my
gifts after the people who give them to me—rather
a nice thought, you know. And I didn't want to
offend anybody in this case, so I called it after the
three of them—Paramount, Warner, Metro-Goldwyn—the first syllable of each—Parwarmet.

GEORGE. Well, won't Fox be sore?

HELEN. Oh, no, Doctor. Because the Fox Studios
gave me a wonderful kennel. And I have twelve
magnificent dogs, all named after Fox executives.
But listen to me rattling on and not asking a word
about *you.* Tell me what you've been doing. And
what in the world took you abroad for eight years?
The last I heard of you——

MAY. *(Quickly)* Yes, I know. Well, of course,
I never expected to stay in the theatre—that is, not
as an actress. I always felt that I was better
equipped to teach. *(Turns to* JERRY.*)*

HELEN. Teach?

MAY. Voice culture. I began with a few private
pupils, and then when I was abroad Lady Tree per-
suaded me to take her on for a while, and from
that I drifted into opening a school, and it's been
very successful. Of course I accept only the very

best people. Mr. Hyland and Doctor Lewis are both associated with me, as I told you. (GEORGE *sits at the mention of his name.*)

HELEN. And now you're going to open a school in Hollywood!

MAY. What? Why, no—we hadn't expected—ah—— *(Turning to* JERRY.*)*

JERRY. Hollywood? We hadn't thought about it.

HELEN. *Wait* till I tell you! Of course you don't know, but something is happening at the present time that is simply going to revolutionize the entire industry. They've finally perfected *talking pictures!*

MAY. No!

HELEN. Yes—and you can't imagine what it's going to *mean.* But here's the point. Every actor and actress in the industry will have to learn to talk, understand? And if *we* were to open the first school,—my *dear!*

MAY. But Helen, we couldn't *think* of such a thing!

JERRY. Oh, no, Miss Hobart!

GEORGE. Sure! That's why we're going—— (JERRY *silences him.*)

HELEN. I simply won't take "No" for an answer!

MAY. But what about our school in London?

JERRY. We've got a good deal of money tied up in London, Miss Hobart.

HELEN. May—America needs you. You're still, I hope, a loyal American?

MAY. Oh, yes, yes. But——

HELEN. Then it's settled. This is Fate, May—our meeting—and in the industry Fate is the only thing we bow to.

MAY. But—— Really, Helen——

HELEN. Now, please—not another word. Oh, but this is marvelous—right at this time. Of course it'll take a certain amount of money to get started, but I know just the man we'll take it to—Herman Glo-gauer! You know—the Glogauer Studios!

MAY. Well, I'm not sure——

JERRY. Oh, yes, of course! } *(Together)*
GEORGE. Yah!

HELEN. I'll send him a telegram, right away, and ask for an appointment.

JERRY. That's a good idea! George! (GEORGE *presses buzzer.)*

MAY. Is he important?

HELEN. Oh, my dear!

JERRY. *Is* he important?

GEORGE. You bet!

HELEN. One of the biggest! And he's the man who first turned down the Vitaphone!

MAY. He did?

HELEN. So he buys *everything* now! You know Mr. Glogauer—— Why, he just signed that famous playwright—you know, May—that Armenian who writes all those wonderful plays and things.

MAY. Noel Coward.

HELEN. That's right. Of course you people can't realize, but a school of voice culture, opening up at this time—well! I should say my half interest alone would bring me in I just don't know how much! *(A look from* MAY *to* JERRY.) Because there's abso-lutely no limit to where the talkies are going—just no limit! Tell me, Doctor—— (GEORGE *fails to re-spond.)* Doctor—— (GEORGE, *spurred on by* JERRY, *pays attention.)* —what do *you* think of this mar-velous development in the motion pictures? Just what is your opinion?

MAY. Well, the Doctor hasn't had much time——

JERRY. He looks after the scientific end.

GEORGE. I think the legitimate stage had better look to its laurels.

HELEN. My words exactly! Just what I've been

saying in my column! *(A look from* MAY *and* JERRY *to* GEORGE, *who suddenly swells with pride.)*

GEORGE. Here is a medium that combines the wide scope of the motion picture with the finer qualities of the stage proper.

HELEN. That's *very* true. May, you've got a great brain here. *(To* GEORGE *again)* I *do* want to talk to you some time, Doctor.

GEORGE. It affords opportunities for entertainment—— (SUSAN WALKER *enters* L. *A young girl about nineteen.)*

HELEN. *(Not stopping)* I want to discuss voice and body control with you.

SUSAN. Oh, hello, Miss Hobart. You said you were coming back, and I waited, and——

HELEN. Yes, dear, but this is very important. I can't talk to you now.

SUSAN. When *can* you talk to me?

HELEN. *(Never giving* SUSAN *a chance to finish)* I'm sure I don't know. Later.

SUSAN. I only want to ask you some questions.

HELEN. I understand, but I'm busy, dear.

SUSAN. Because you could be of such help to me.

HELEN. *Yes,* dear.

GEORGE. *(Who has been showing a growing interest)* Wouldn't you like to sit down?

(WARN Curtain.)

SUSAN. Oh, thank you. I——

HELEN. *(Compelled to introduce her)* This is little Miss—ah——

SUSAN. Susan Walker.

HELEN. Susan Walker. She's the little girl I was telling you about.

GEORGE. *(To* SUSAN*)* Are you going to act in pictures?

HELEN. She wants to—yes. Tell me, Doctor——

SUSAN. I'm going to try to, if I can get started. I don't know very much about it.

HELEN. *(In* SUSAN's *tone)* She doesn't know very much about it.

GEORGE. You could go to our school! May!

SUSAN. What?

HELEN. Yes, yes, of course. Now run along, dear, and read the Book of the Month or something. We're very busy.

SUSAN. Well, but you *will* let me talk to you later, won't you?

HELEN. Yes, of course, dear.

SUSAN. Goodbye. *(Her glance sweeps the* OTHERS; *rests timidly on* GEORGE *for a second.)*

GEORGE. Are you right in the next car?

SUSAN. No, I'm in Number Twenty—with my mother.

HELEN. She's with her mother.

GEORGE. I'll take you back, if you want.

MAY. Yes, you do that, George. That'll be fine.

SUSAN. Oh, thank you very much.

HELEN. *(As* GEORGE *crosses to* SUSAN*)* You won't stay long, will you, Doctor? Because I want to hear more of your ideas. I can see that you've given it thought.

GEORGE. *(Piloting* SUSAN *out)* No, I'll be right —that is, unless—— *(He takes refuge in turning to* SUSAN*)* What's your mother's name? Mrs. Walker? *(Exit* GEORGE *and* SUSAN L.*)*

HELEN. What a man! He must have been enormous in England!

MAY. Very big! Wasn't he?

JERRY. Yes, indeed!

HELEN. May, *do* you think we can keep him in America?

MAY. Jerry, can we keep him in America?

JERRY. I think we can keep him in America.

MAY. I guess we can keep him in America——

(The CURTAIN starts down medium slow. The train WHISTLE is heard.)

HELEN. Marvelous! How much
would it cost, May, to start things going?   }
JERRY. Fifty thousand!   } *(Together)*
MAY. A hundred thousand!

HELEN. Oh, that's more like it. Be-
cause Mr. Glogauer is a big man and
he does things in a big way!   }
JERRY. I guess you're right, May.   } *(Together)*
It would cost a hundred thousand——
MAY. It would take at least that——   }

HELEN. Now, we get to Hollywood on Thursday—— *(All* THREE *are talking excitedly, simultaneously, as the CURTAIN falls.)*

ACT ONE

SCENE III

SCENE: *The Gold Room of the Hotel Stilton, Los Angeles. Double doors R. and L., opening off-stage. An arch up C., to which two steps lead, with a balcony beyond, overlooking the dining room and dance floor. A settee and end table R.C., another L.C. At the raked corner up R. and up L., console tables and small stools; lamps on the tables. Side chairs below doors R. and L. The room is gaudy and ornate in the extreme. An offstage orchestra plays "Sonny Boy" continuously throughout the scene.*

(FIRST COUPLE *enters from* L *and cross upstage to* R.)

FIRST MAN. So I said to him, "Listen, what's there to be scared of? They'll still need scenario writers."

(SECOND COUPLE *enter from* R. *and cross downstage. The two scenes are played simultaneously*)

FIRST GIRL. Well, I think you've very good. I liked that last picture of yours an awful lot

SECOND MAN. What's the use of your meeting him? The part isn't your type. This girl is eigh-

31

First Man. Oh, that wasn't anything. Wait till you see my next one.

First Girl. Oh, I'm just crazy to! *(They exit to* R.*)*

(A Man *enters from* R.; *crosses downstage.)*

teen years old and a virgin.

Second Girl. I look eighteen under lights and I can talk like a virgin.

Second Man. Oh, all right. I'll have you meet him if you want to. But it won't do any good.

Second Girl. Listen, if I meet him it will do some good. *(They are off* L.*)*

(A Cigarette Girl, *dressed in Spanish costume, and humming "Sonny Boy," enters from* L. *As the* Second Couple *exit* L., *a* Coat Check Girl *enters* L.*)*

Cigarette Girl. *(Who has crossed above the settee, to the* Man *who has entered* R. *and is crossing downstage)* Cigars, cigarettes! *(He shakes his head and continues without stopping, leaving the* Cigarette Girl *and the* Coat Check Girl *alone.)*

Coat Check Girl. Say, I got a tip for you, Kate.

Cigarette Girl. Yah?

Coat Check Girl. I was out to Universal today. I heard they was going to do a shipwreck picture.

Cigarette Girl. Not enough sound. They're making it a college picture—glee clubs.

Coat Check Girl. That was this morning. It's French Revolution now.

Cigarette Girl. Yah? There ought to be something it that for me.

Coat Check Girl. Sure! There's a call out for prostitutes for Wednesday.

Cigarette Girl. Say, I'm going out there! Remember that prostitute I did for Paramount?

COAT CHECK GIRL. Yah, but that was silent. This is for talking prostitutes. *(She drops into a respectful silence as* PHYLLIS FONTAINE *and* FLORABEL LEIGH *enter. They are movie stars—ermined and orchided to the ears. They are followed by* TWO MAIDS, *each carrying an extra ermine wrap, and the* MAIDS, *in turn, are followed by* TWO CHAUFFEURS, *each with an automobile robe. The* CIGARETTE *and* COAT CHECK GIRLS *greet them with a mumbled* "Good evening, Miss Fontaine" *and* "Good evening, Miss Leigh." *They receive little nods in reply.)*

FIRST CHAUFFEUR. Is the staircase clear?

COAT CHECK GIRL. Yes, it is.

FIRST CHAUFFEUR. *(To* FIRST MAID*)* The staircase is clear.

FIRST MAID. The staircase is clear, Miss Leigh.

SECOND MAID. The staircase is clear, Miss Fontaine. *(At a gesture from their* MISTRESSES, *the* TWO MAIDS *assist them to slip out of their respective ermine wraps, and in their place they substitute the spares.)*

FLORABEL. *(Exiting* L.*)* If they put us at that back table I'm going to raise an awful stink.

PHYLLIS. *(Following)* Yes, goddam it, they ought to know by this time—— (PHYLLIS *and* FLORABEL *exit* L. MAIDS *and* CHAUFFEURS *remain behind.)*

FIRST MAID. *(To* CIGARETTE GIRL*)* Hello.

CIGARETTE GIRL. Hello.

FIRST CHAUFFEUR. You girls working this week?

CIGARETTE GIRL. No, we ain't.

SECOND CHAUFFEUR. Universal's doing a college picture. (MAIDS *and* CHAUFFEURS *have crossed to door* R. *A* BELLBOY *enters* L.*)*

BELLBOY. Say, I hear you boys are all set out at Universal. French Revolution picture.

SECOND CHAUFFEUR. No, they changed it. It's a college picture.

BELLBOY. It's Revolution again—they just changed it back down in the Men's Room.

CIGARETTE GIRL. Oh, that's good.

BELLBOY. Yah, on account of the sound. The sound, you know. They're going to be playing the guillotine all through. *(He strums an imaginary banjo.)*

SECOND MAID. That means I'm out of it.

FIRST CHAUFFEUR. You can't tell—

SECOND MAID. I don't know one note from another. *(Together)*

FIRST MAID. Me too.

SECOND CHAUFFEUR. Let's see what it is in the morning. *(The* MAIDS *and* CHAUFFEURS *are out,* R.*)* *(Together)*

BELLBOY. What do you think happened about five minutes ago? I was down in the Men's Room—singing—and Mr. Katzenstein came in.

COAT CHECK GIRL. That's a break!

CIGARETTE GIRL. Did he hear you?

BELLBOY. You bet he heard me. Said I had a great voice and told me to come and see him.

CIGARETTE GIRL. Say—— *(Exits* L.*)*

BELLBOY. What do you think of that? *(Exits* L.*)*

COAT CHECK GIRL. Gosh, I wish he'd come into the ladies' room. *(Exit* CIGARETTE GIRL, COAT CHECK GIRL, BELLBOY, L., *just as* SUSAN *enters* R. *She runs on excitedly.)*

SUSAN. *(Hurrying to balcony)* Mother! Come on! Hurry up!

MRS. WALKER. Yes, dear. *(Enters* R.*)*

SUSAN. This is wonderful here! Look! *(She hurries to the railing,* MRS. WALKER *following)* There's where they're all going to eat! *(*MAN *crosses* R. *to* L., *whistling.)*

MRS. WALKER. Yes, dear. Don't over-excite yourself.

SUSAN. But, Mother, imagine! Practically every big star in Hollywood will be there.

MRS. WALKER. *(Following her downstage)* Yes, I know, dear.

SUSAN. This is where they come every Wednesday. They're—they're all over the place now. *(Coming downstage, looking off L. Excitedly)* Look! Can you recognize anyone?

MRS. WALKER. *(Looking)* Isn't that John Gilbert?

SUSAN. Where? Where?

MRS. WALKER. Over there! Right near that post.

SUSAN. Mother! That's a waiter!

MRS. WALKER. *(Crossing to below the settee L.)* Well, I'm sure I don't know how one is to tell. Every man we see looks more and more like John Gilbert.

SUSAN. Well—we'll see some of the real ones tonight, Mother. Doctor Lewis said we're sure to see everyone.

MRS. WALKER. If there're so many people trying to be picture actors, I'm afraid they'll never give *you* a chance.

SUSAN. Oh, but it's different now——

(ERNEST, the headwaiter, enters R., crosses to above the settee R., stops, and poses for a moment as SUSAN and MRS. WALKER gaze admiringly. He starts upstage as a MAN (NORTON) and a WOMAN enter L. and cross above the settee.)

NORTON. I just saw her downstairs. Wouldn't you think, after the preview of that last picture, she'd stay home and hide? *(As they reach just L. of C. NORTON notices ERNEST)* Oh, Ernest!

ERNEST. Yes, Mr. Norton.

NORTON. I'm expecting some guests—two gentlemen and a lady. Will you see that they're brought to my table?

ERNEST. Yes, sir. Very good, sir. (SUSAN *and* MRS. WALKER *exchange looks of disappointment.* NORTON *and the* WOMAN *continue* R., *talking as they go, and* ERNEST *comes down to* SUSAN *and* MRS. WALKER. *The* WOMAN *and* NORTON *continue their conversation simultaneously with the scene between* ERNEST, SUSAN *and* MRS. WALKER *until they are offstage.)*

WOMAN. Who is the man that came over to Diane's table? Must be one of her new ones, eh?

NORTON. Must be.

WOMAN. I give him just about three weeks. *(They exit* R.*)*

ERNEST. *(As he comes downstage after talking to* NORTON*)* Anything I can do for you, Madam?

MRS. WALKER. Why, no, I guess not.

SUSAN. Have any of the stars arrived yet?

ERNEST. Very few, Miss. It's only nine-thirty. There are one or two cowboy stars here, but I don't suppose you'd be interested in them.

SUSAN. Oh, no.

MRS. WALKER. I don't like Westerns very much.

ERNEST. Of course no one of any consequence gets here before ten. You get a smattering of First National and Pathe about nine-thirty, but you don't get United Artists until ten-fifteen.

SUSAN. But they'll all *be* here, won't they?

ERNEST. Oh, yes. Everyone who is of any importance in the industry comes here every Wednesday night.

MRS. WALKER. My, you must find it interesting!

ERNEST. Yes, you get *life* out here. In fact, I get most of the ideas for my scenarios right here in the hotel.

SUSAN. Scenarios? Mother, he's a scenario writer!

MRS. WALKER. Really?

ERNEST. I dabble a bit, that's all.

SUSAN. Have you had any produced? Who was in them?

ERNEST. Well, Paramount is dickering for something of mine right now.

SUSAN. Mother, did you hear that? Paramount is dickering!

MRS. WALKER. It is? *(Together)*
SUSAN. How proud you must feel!

ERNEST. Well, of course, one never knows.

SUSAN. But to have Paramount dickering!

SUSAN. Who is the story for? I hope it's Greta Garbo. *(Together)*
MRS. WALKER. It's wonderful!

ERNEST. Miss Garbo's all right, but—— *(Breaks off as he sees someone offstage; crosses up C. to get a better view.)*

SUSAN. Who is it?

ERNEST. I *think*—yes, it is! It's Buddy Rogers!

MRS. WALKER. Really? Where? *(Together)*
SUSAN. It is?

ERNEST. You're very lucky, ladies. Only nine forty-five, and you've got Buddy Rogers.

SUSAN *and* MRS. WALKER. *(As they exit L.)* O-o-oh! *(As* ERNEST *starts to follow them out,* METERSTEIN *and* MISS CHASEN *enter from R. and cross upstage.)*

METERSTEIN. So I said to Katzenstein, "Why don't we buy it? It's the biggest thing in New York today. 'Strange Interlude'! And look at the name you get! Eugene O'Neill!" (GEORGE *enters R. and takes in the scene.)*

MISS CHASEN. Well, did he write the music, too?

(The SECOND COUPLE *who were seen at the opening of the scene enter from L. and cross downstage. The* TWO COUPLES *talk simultaneously.)*

METERSTEIN. No, he just did the libretto. But if we can get him out here I've got a great guy to team him up with. He's a little Jewish fellow—— *(They exit* L.*)*

(GEORGE, *a little taken aback by this, crosses to down* R.C. *The* CIGARETTE GIRL *enters* L., *unseen by* GEORGE.)

CIGARETTE GIRL. *(Coming close to* GEORGE, *her voice turning him toward her. In the well-known Garbo manner)* Will—you have—some—cigarettes?

GEORGE. *(Scared)* Why —no.

SECOND GIRL. Why didn't you introduce me to him? I just stood there like a fool.

SECOND MAN. It wasn't the right moment. I'll take you to him when they're ready to cast the picture.

SECOND GIRL. Oh, it wasn't? Well, you're coming right downstairs and over to his table and introduce me as the best goddam actress in Hollywood!

SECOND MAN. Now, listen, honey. You know I want you to get the part. *(They exit* R.*)*

CIGARETTE GIRL. *(Acting to beat the band, and beating it seven to three)* Very well. I'm—sorry— I—intruded. *(Exits* L. GEORGE *decides to get out of there. Before he can reach the door* R. SUSAN *re-enters* L.*.)*

SUSAN. Hello, George.

GEORGE. *(Returning)* Oh, hello.

SUSAN. Isn't it exciting? Seeing all the stars and everything!

GEORGE. I should say so!

SUSAN. I left Mother at the staircase, watching them all walk down. Hollywood is even better than I dreamed it would be! Aren't you crazy about it?

GEORGE. It's wonderful, all right. It kinda re-

minds me of the first time I went to the circus—
only there's no elephants.

SUSAN. I can hardly wait till I become a star—
when I can do the things they do, and have myself
pointed out to tourists.

GEORGE. I'll tell you something, Susan, if you
promise not to breathe it. Who do you think we're
going to meet here tonight?

SUSAN. Who?

GEORGE. Herman Glogauer, one of the biggest
motion picture producers in the country.

SUSAN. Really? Oh, George, will you tell him
about me—see if he'll give me a part?

GEORGE. Sure. That's what I'm meeting him for.
(MRS. WALKER *enters* L. *The* THREE *are standing
down* C.)

SUSAN. Oh, George!

MRS. WALKER. Susan, I just saw——

SUSAN. Mother, what do you think? Doctor Lewis
is meeting Herman Glogauer here tonight and he's
going to tell him all about me!

GEORGE. Hello, Mrs. Walker.

MRS. WALKER. Well, isn't that fine? A big man
like that coming here to talk about Susan!

SUSAN. Where's he going to be? Right here?

GEORGE. Yes.

SUSAN. Will you introduce me to him?

MRS. WALKER. You just leave it to Doctor Lewis,
dear.

GEORGE. I think you'd be just great in talkies—
the way you recite and everything. I told May all
about those poems you recited. Especially that one—
What was it?

MRS. WALKER. "Boots"? By Rudyard Kipling?

GEORGE. Yes, that's it.

SUSAN. (*To a pedal accompaniment*) "Boots,
boots, boots, boots, movin' up and down again. Five,
seven, nine, eleven——"

GEORGE. *(Trying to stop her)* Yeah, yeah, that's it—that's it—— Yah—that's the one. (SUSAN *stops.)* She told me she sort of felt Susan recited "Boots" from the minute she laid eyes on you. Does she do that one about "It Takes a Heap of Loving to——"

SUSAN. "To Make a House a Home"? Oh, yes.

MRS. WALKER. That's one of her best.

GEORGE. Miss Daniels said you probably did. She felt a lot more things about you, too. I guess she's pretty interested.

MRS. WALKER. Would she want to give her an audition?

GEORGE. I don't think she'll have to. I told her how Susan made me feel—when that man in the poem goes crazy, how I felt sort of weak myself—and she said she wouldn't want to take a chance.

MRS. WALKER. You've been wonderful to us, Doctor. I'd just trust Susan anywhere with you—I told her today I thought you were the most harmless motion picture man in the business. (MAY *and* JERRY *enter* R.)

MAY. Good evening! What's going on here?

MRS. WALKER. Hello, Miss Daniels. Hello, Mr. Hyland.

GEORGE. Oh, May! Susan does know that poem about living in a house or something.

MAY. Sure she does. She knows "Ring Out, Wild Bells," too, don't you, Susan?

SUSAN. Oh, yes.

MRS. WALKER. That was one of her first ones. } *(Together)*

MAY. *(To* JERRY*)* That's five you owe me.

JERRY. Huh?

MRS. WALKER. Well, come on, Susan. We'll get on out. We know you're going to meet Mr. Glogauer.

MAY. *(Very sweetly)* Oh, did George tell you we're going to meet Mr. Glogauer?

SUSAN. Oh, yes.   } *(Together)*
JERRY. Isn't that fine? }

GEORGE. I just mentioned it.

MRS. WALKER. I think it's just wonderful what Doctor Lewis has accomplished.

MAY. How's that?

MRS. WALKER. Just wonderful!

SUSAN. Goodbye.

GEORGE. Goodbye.

MAY. Take care of yourselves. *(Exit SUSAN and MRS. WALKER L.)* Jerry!

JERRY. Huh?

MAY. Would there be some way of making him silent as well as dumb?

GEORGE. I didn't hurt anything.

JERRY. Well, kid, here it is! Hollywood! And was I right? Did you hear 'em downstairs? Scared stiff!

MAY. *(Sitting settee R.)* Not nearly as scared as I am.

JERRY. All we got to do is play our cards right. This is the time and place. Chance to make a million or lose a million.

MAY. Which do you think we ought to do?

JERRY. If things go right for us, May, it won't be long now. And we'll do it in style, too.

GEORGE. What do you mean, Jerry—that you and May are going to get married? Are you, May?

MAY. Look, George, we've got all kinds of things on our mind. You'll be the first to know.

JERRY. Yes, sir, it's all up to how we click with Glogauer—and we'll click with him, too!

GEORGE. He's pretty lucky we came out here.

MAY. *(Crossing L. to GEORGE)* George, when Mr. Glogauer gets here and you're introduced to him, just say, "Hello." See? In a pinch, "Hello, Mr. Glogauer." Then from that time on—nothing.

GEORGE. Yeah! But suppose I have a good idea? Huh?

MAY. That's when I sing "Aida."

JERRY. Say, Glogauer ought to be getting here. Where's Helen?

MAY. Down talking terms with a couple of hundred movie stars. I was out at Parwarmet today. Only twenty-two rooms—just a shack, really.

JERRY. *That* part's all right. She's been damned nice to us.

MAY. Sure. For fifty percent of the gross she'd be damned nice to Mae West.

GIRLS. *(Voices off R.)* Oh, Miss Hobart, may we see you a minute——?

HELEN. *(Entering R.)* Not now, dears. *(To MAY and JERRY)* My dear, *everyone* is here tonight. And such excitement! Nobody knows where they're at. *(There are greetings from the THREE, which HELEN, in her excitement, rides right over)* And of course, wherever you turn all you hear is sound. One has to be very careful whom one insults these days— they may be the very ones to survive.

MAY. Things are pretty well topsy-turvy, aren't they?

HELEN. I should say so! What do you think I just heard? You know that tremendous spectacle the Schlepkin Brothers are putting on—"The Old Testament"? Well, Mr. Schlepkin—I mean the oldest of the twelve brothers—the real brains of the business—he used to have the cloakroom privilege in all the West Coast theatres—he just told me that they've stopped work on the picture and they're scrapping the whole thing. They're not going to make anything but talkies from now on.

JERRY. Big people, the Schlepkins. I'd like to meet them.

MAY. Are they all here tonight?

HELEN. Oh, all twelve of them. That shows you what they think of the talkies—it's the first time in years that they've all been in Hollywood at the same time. They generally keep two with their mother—she lives in Brooklyn and they fly back and forth. Such a lovely thought! Why, their aeroplane bill alone is ten thousand dollars a month.

(BELLBOY *and* POLICEMEN *enter from* L. *March across upstage.*)

HELEN. Oh, Mr. Glogauer must be coming now. *(To* BELLBOY*)* Is that for Mr. Glogauer?

BELLBOY. Yes, Miss Hobart. His car just drew up. (BELLBOY *and* POLICEMEN *exit* R.*)*

HELEN. They always give him an escort, so he can get through the lobby. If he says "yes" to our little proposition we can turn this into a celebration.

MAY. It's marvelous you were able to get him to come.

JERRY. Yes, indeed.

HELEN. Oh, they'll all come running now. Even the big ones. Besides, Glogauer is scared stiff. He's the man who first turned down the Vitaphone—I told you.

MAY. Oh, yes.

HELEN. Anyhow, that's the story. Of course, he's never admitted it, and no one's ever *dared* mention it to him.

JERRY. I wouldn't think so.

GEORGE. *(Ever literal)* What did he turn it down for?

HELEN. *(Crossing to him)* He just didn't know, Doctor, what it was going to amount to. He didn't have enough vision.

GIRL. *(Entering* L.*)* Oh, Miss Hobart——

HELEN. *(Crossing to her)* No, dear, not now.

Later on, maybe. *(She waves the* GIRL *out)* Someone wanted to meet the Doctor.

GEORGE. What?

HELEN. Oh, I lost no time, Doctor, in telling them
about you. Isn't it marvelous, May—— *(A* CROWD
is heard off R., *which surges on stage, bearing* GLO-
GAUER *with it.)* Oh, here he is now—— *(*HELEN
crosses to R.*)*

*(A rising NOISE offstage has interrupted her. Any
 number of VOICES are saying, "Mr. Glogauer! Mr. Glogauer!"* HERMAN GLOGAUER
 *enters, followed by a streaming and screaming
 MOB, which the* BELLBOY *and the* POLICE *are
 trying to hold in check.)*

HELEN. *(To* MAY *and* JERRY*)* Here he is now!

GLOGAUER. *(As he enters)* No, no, no, no! I
can't see anyone now! No one!

HELEN. *(Through the commotion)* Well, well,
here's the great man himself. And on time, too.

BELLBOY. *(Has entered with* GLOGAUER; *now
pushes back the* CROWD*)* Mr. Glogauer can't see
anyone. Please go on out.

GLOGAUER. That's it. Close the door. Let's have
a little peace here.

HELEN. *(As the doors close and the NOISE subsides)* Mr. Glogauer, this is Miss Daniels, Mr. Hyland, and Doctor Lewis. *(They murmur acknowl-
edgements.)*

GLOGAUER. How are you?

BELLBOY. *(Who is standing at door with* POLICE-
MEN*)* Mr. Glogauer!

GLOGAUER. Yes—what is it?

BELLBOY. Are you in the market for a great trio?

GLOGAUER. What? *(*BELLBOY *and* POLICEMEN *immediately burst into "Pale hands I loved——" They
get just about that much out.)*

GLOGAUER. *(Wincing)* No, no, no! Nothing! Go away! *(The* BELLBOY *and* POLICEMEN *go out* R. *reluctantly. You hear the* CROWD *as the door opens.)*

MAY. What's all that about?

GLOGAUER. These people!

HELEN. You see, they all know Mr. Glogauer, and they try to show him they can act.

GLOGAUER. It's terrible! Terrible! Everywhere I go they act at me. Everyone acts at me! If I only go to have my shoes shined, I look down and someone is having a love scene with my pants.

HELEN. That's the penalty of being so big a man.

GLOGAUER. All over the hotel they come at me. Ordinarily I would say, "Let's go out to my house, where we got some peace." But Mrs. Glogauer is having new fountains put in the entrance hall.

HELEN. It's the most gorgeous house, May. You remember—we saw it from the train.

MAY. Oh, yes. With the illuminated dome.

HELEN. And the turrets.

GLOGAUER. In gold leaf.

HELEN. But the *inside,* May! I want you to see his bathroom! You must see his bathroom!

MAY. I can hardly wait.

HELEN. It's the show place of Hollywood! But they can see it some other time—can't they, Mr. Glogauer?

GLOGAUER. Any Wednesday. There is a guide there from two to five. I tell you what you do. Phone my secretary—I send my car for you.

MAY. Why, that'll be wonderful.

HELEN. Yes, and what a car it is! It's a Rolls-Royce!

MAY. You don't say?

GEORGE. What year?

JERRY. *(Coming to the rescue)* Well, Mr. Glogauer, we understand that you're in the midst of quite a revolution out here.

HELEN. I should say he is!

GLOGAUER. Is it a revolution? And who have we got to thank for it? The Schlepkin Brothers. What did they have to go and make pictures talk for? Things were going along fine. You couldn't stop making money—even if you turned out a *good* picture you made money.

JERRY. There is no doubt about it—the entire motion picture is on the verge of a new era.

HELEN. Mr. Glogauer, I tell you the talkies are here to stay.

GEORGE. *(Rises; crosses to join the* GROUP*)* The legitimate stage had better——

MAY. All right, George. (GEORGE *cracks nut as he retires to settee* L.*)*

GLOGAUER. Sure, sure! It's colossal! A fellow sings a couple of songs at 'em and everybody goes crazy! Those lucky bums!

HELEN. He means the Schlepkin Brothers.

GLOGAUER. Four times already they were on their last legs and every time they got new ones. Everything comes to those Schlepkin Brothers! This fellow Lou Jackson—sings these mammies or whatever it is—he comes all the way across the country and goes right to the Schlepkin Brothers.

BELLBOY. *(Enters* R.*)* I beg your pardon, Mr. Glogauer?

GLOGAUER. Yes, yes? What is it?

BELLBOY. The twelve Schlepkin Brothers would like to talk to you. They're downstairs.

GLOGAUER. Tell 'em later on. I come down later.

BELLBOY. Yes, sir. *(Goes off* R.*)*

GLOGAUER. Schlepkin Brothers! I know what they want! They're sitting on top of the world now —with their Lou Jackson—so they try to gobble up everybody! All my life they been trying to get me. Way back in the fur business already, when I had nickelodeons and they only had pennylodeons. Always wanting to merge, merge! And because there's twelve of them they want odds yet!

JERRY. But you can teach your own people to talk. Why not let us take them in hand and give them back to you perfect in the use of the English language?

HELEN. I told you about their school in London— Lady Tree——

MAY. It's entirely a matter of correct breathing, Mr. Glogauer. Abdominal respiration is the key-note of elocutionary training.

JERRY. We'll not only teach your people to talk, Mr. Glogauer, but we'll have them talking as well as you do.

GLOGAUER. Well, I don't ask miracles.

BELLBOY. *(Enters R.)* Mr. Glogauer!

GLOGAUER. Well? Well? What now?

BELLBOY. The Schlepkin Brothers are flying to Brooklyn in half an hour. They say they've got to see you right away.

GLOGAUER. Tell 'em in a minute. And tell Phyllis Fontaine and Florabel Leigh I want to see 'em up here right away. *(To the* OTHERS*)* Two of my biggest stars. *(To the* BELLBOY*)* Tell 'em to come up alone—without any of the Schlepkin Brothers.

BELLBOY. Yes, sir. *(Goes R.)*

GEORGE. Excuse me—I'll be right back. *(Dashes off L.)*

GLOGAUER. Phyllis Fontaine—seventy-five hundred dollars a week she draws down. And in the old days she was worth it! Every time she undressed in a picture it was sure fire!

HELEN. The most beautiful legs in America!

GLOGAUER. But you can't hear 'em! You know what I do now? The biggest stage actress in America I am bringing out—from New York. Ten thousand a week I'm paying her! I never heard of her before. (PHYLLIS *and* FLORABEL *enter* L.)

PHYLLIS *and* FLORABEL. *(In those awful voices)*
Hello, Hermie.

GLOGAUER. Ah, here we are, girls! This is the
ladies I was telling you about. Phyllis Fontaine and
Florabel Leigh.

HELEN. Hello, darlings!

FLORABEL. Hello, Helen!

GLOGAUER. Listen, girls—this is Miss Daniels and
Mr. Hyland—voice specialists from England.

PHYLLIS. Voice specialists! ⎫
FLORABEL. Whaddye know? ⎭ *(Together)*

GLOGAUER. Well, here they are, Miss Daniels.
This is what I'm up against.

MAY. I'd like to listen to their breathing, if I
may, Mr. Glogauer.

HELEN. You know, it's all a question of breathing.

JERRY. That's the whole story.

MAY. May I ask if you ladies have ever breathed
rhythmically?

PHYLLIS. What? ⎫
FLORABEL. Why, not that I know of. ⎭ *(Together)*

MAY. You see, rhythmic breathing is the basis of
all tonal quality.

JERRY. It's the keynote.

MAY. If you are able to breathe rhythmically
then there is every reason to beiieve that you will be
able to talk correctly.

HELEN. That's right!

GLOGAUER. Well—what about it? *(To the GIRLS)*
Can you do it?

MAY. *(As the GIRLS look blank)* If you'll per-
mit me, I think I can tell you.

GLOGAUER. *(Impressed)* Sure, sure. *(There is an
impressive silence as MAY goes to FLORABEL and
puts her head to her chest.)*

MAY. Will you breathe, please?

FLORABEL. Yes, ma'am. (MAY *raises her head. They expect some word. The suspense is terrific.*)

GLOGAUER. Well?

HELEN. Sssh! (MAY *passes on to* PHYLLIS; *repeats the operation.*)

MAY. Please breathe. (PHYLLIS *gives her a terrified look.*) (*WARN Curtain.*)

GLOGAUER. (*When it is over*) Well? How about it? (MAY *nods sagely.*) We got something?

MAY (*Quietly*) Absolutely.

HELEN. Isn't that wonderful?}
PHYLLIS. We can do it?   } (*Together*)

GLOGAUER. Keep still, girls! We got something, huh? We ain't licked yet? What's next? What do they do now?

MAY. For the present they should just keep breathing.

GLOGAUER. Hear that, girls? Wait around—don't go home. (*He motions them out of the way.* FLORABEL *sits settee* L. PHYLLIS *stands above settee.*) Now I tell you how we handle this! I give you rooms right in the studio and as fast as you turn 'em out we put 'em right to work! We got to work fast, remember?

JERRY. Right! }
MAY. Right! } (*Together*)

GLOGAUER. You teach these people to talk and it's worth all the money in the world!

JERRY. We'll teach 'em.

GLOGAUER. (*Barely stopping*) You people came out here just in time! We'll show 'em with their Lou Jackson! This is a lifesaver. (GEORGE *rushes on* L. *with* SUSAN.) To hell with the Schlepkin Brothers!

GEORGE. There he is, Susan! Right there!

SUSAN. (*Goes up to* GLOGAUER; *turns him around to face her*) "Boots" by Rudyard Kipiing.

GLOGAUER. What?

SUSAN. *(Starts reciting, and continues until the Curtain is down)* "Boots, boots, boots——" (BELLBOY *enters* R.)

GLOGAUER. What do you mean, "Boots"? I don't want any boots. What are you talking about?

SUSAN. *(Continuing)* "——moving up and down again——"

BELLBOY. *(Announcing through* GLOGAUER'S *speech)* The twelve Schlepkin Brothers!

(The TWELVE SCHLEPKIN BROTHERS *start to march on from* R., *two abreast.)*

SENIOR SCHLEPKIN BROTHER. Listen, Herman— we're flying back to New York tonight——

(As the first FOUR SCHLEPKINS *get on stage the Curtain starts to fall.* SUSAN *is still reciting.)*

GLOGAUER. No, sir! I wouldn't merge! I got something better! I wouldn't merge!

THE CURTAIN IS DOWN

ACT TWO

SCENE: *The reception room at the Glogauer Studio.*
Ultra modernistic in its decorations, the room is
meant to impress visitors, and it seldom falls
short of its purpose. The walls are draped in
heavy blue plush, the lighting fixtures are fan-
tastic, and the furniture is nobody's business. It
is the sort of room that could only happen as
the reception room in a leading motion picture
studio. So far as practical purposes are con-
cerned, it might be noted that there are four
doors, R.1 and R.2, L.1 and L.2, that lead into it,
and that the furniture includes one desk, L., be-
tween the upstage and downstage doors—mod-
ernistic as possible, but a desk. It belongs to
the RECEPTION SECRETARY.

LAWRENCE VAIL, *a slim, black-haired young*
man, is discovered waiting, not too comfortably,
in one of the modernistic chairs, R. of the door
up R.2. He is sunk deep down in his chair and
wears the hunted look of a man who has been
waiting for days and days—and is still waiting.
At the desk sits the RECEPTION SECRETARY,
languidly examining this paper and that. She
is pretty much like the furniture. She wears a
flowing black evening gown, although it is early
morning, fondles a long string of pearls, and be-
haves very much like Elinor Glyn.

At the rise of the Curtain MISS CHASEN *en-*

ters with papers, R.1, *goes to the* RECEPTION
SECRETARY, *whose name is* MISS LEIGHTON.
The PHONE rings.

MISS LEIGHTON. *(At phone)* Miss Leighton at
this end.
MISS CHASEN. *(Putting her papers down)* Requi-
sition Department!
MISS LEIGHTON. Requisitions right!

(METERSTEIN *and* WEISSKOPF *enter* R.2. MISS
CHASEN *exits* L.2. *This conversation is carried
on simultaneously with* MISS LEIGHTON'S *phone
talk.)*

WEISSKOPF. But the important thing is your re-
takes.
METERSTEIN. That's it—your retakes. (OFFICE
GIRL *enters* R.2; *exits* R.1.)
WEISSKOPF. You take your retakes, and if they
aren't good you've got no picture.
METERSTEIN. Oh, it's the retakes.
WEISSKOPF. Yeh, it's the retakes, all right. *(They
are gone,* L.1.)
MISS LEIGHTON. *(On phone through all this)*
I shall have to consult the Option Department——
Oh, no, all options are taken care of by the Option
Department—— That would be Mr. Fleming of the
Option Department—— Correct! *(Hangs up. There
is quiet for a second.* 1ST PAGE *enters* L.2 *with a
sign reading, "MR. GLOGAUER IS ON NUM-
BER FOUR." He clicks his heels, shows the sign
to* MISS LEIGHTON, *then to* VAIL; *exits* L.2. *The
PHONE rings. At the phone)* Miss Leighton at
this end—— Who?—Oh, yes. Yes, he knows you're
waiting.—How many days?—Well, I'm afraid you'll
just have to wait—— What?—Oh, no, you couldn't
possibly see Mr. Glogauer—— No, I can't make an

appointment for you. Mr. Weisskopf makes all Mr. Glogauer's appointments—— Oh, no, you can't see Mr. Weisskopf—— You can only see Mr. Weisskopf through Mr. Meterstein—— Oh, no, no one ever sees Mr. Meterstein. *(She hangs up.)*

(2ND PAGE enters L.2 with a sign reading, "MR. WEISSKOPF IS ON NUMBER EIGHT." He stops L. of and a little above the table, clicks his heels, and shows the sign to VAIL, which VAIL acknowledges, then exits L.2. The 1ST PAGE enters from L.1 with some slips of paper which he gives to MISS LEIGHTON.)

1ST PAGE. Waiting to see Miss Daniels.
MISS LEIGHTON. Miss Daniels is still busy with the ten-o'clock class. Take them into Number Six. I will be there in three minutes.
1ST PAGE. Number Six in three minutes. Yes, Miss Leighton. *(He exits L.2.)*

(ART SULLIVAN and VICTOR MOULTON enter L.1.)

SULLIVAN. Get it? She makes believe she's falling for this rich bozo—to save her sister, do you see?— *and the show goes on.* Plenty of spots for numbers in the revue scenes—— *(To MISS LEIGHTON)* Are they ready for us, Sister?
MISS LEIGHTON. Waiting for you, Mr. Sullivan. Number Ten.
SULLIVAN. *(Hardly stopping)* And the kid sister thinks she's double-crossing her. Of course she sees her kissing this fellow——
OLIVER FULTON. *(Another author, enters L.1)* Hello, boys.
SULLIVAN. Hello, Ollie—you're just in time. They're waiting to hear it.
FULTON. O.K. *(Starts up.)*

SULLIVAN. Wait till I tell you the new twist. She makes believe she's falling for the rich guy—for her sister's sake, get it?

FULTON. And the show goes on! For God's sake, Art, I told you that at lunch yesterday.

SULLIVAN. Did you?

FULTON. I don't mind your stealing from Fox or Metro—that's legitimate—but if we steal our own stuff we'll never know where we are. (*Exit* FULTON, MOULTON *and* SULLIVAN, L.2. *PHONE rings.*)

MISS LEIGHTON. Miss Leighton at this end—— No, Miss Daniels is still with the ten o'clock class— Oh, no, the lisp and nasal throat toners are at one— Didn't you receive the notification?—I'll have Miss Daniels' secretary send you one—— You're welcome. (*Hangs up.* 2ND PAGE *enters* L.2 *on "notification" with sign,* "MR. GLOGAUER IS ON NUMBER NINE." *Exhibits it; exits* L.2. MISS LEIGHTON *finally notices* VAIL) I beg your pardon, but I forget whom you're waiting to see.

VAIL. I don't wonder.

MISS LEIGHTON. I beg your pardon.

VAIL. I am waiting to see Mr. Glogauer.

MISS LEIGHTON. Mr. Glogauer is on Number Nine.

VAIL. Napoleon just informed me.

MISS LEIGHTON. How's that?

VAIL. It isn't important.

MISS LEIGHTON. (*Rises; crosses to up* C.) Have you an appointment with Mr. Glogauer?

VAIL. Yes, ma'am—direct. Right through Mr. Meterstein to Mr. Weisskopf to Mr. Glogauer.

MISS LEIGHTON. If you'll give me your name I'll tell Mr. Weisskopf.

VAIL. My name is Lawrence Vail. I gave it to you yesterday, and the day before that, and the day—— I would like to see Mr. Glogauer. (*PHONE rings.*)

MISS LEIGHTON. I'll tell Mr. Weisskopf.

VAIL. I'm ever so much obliged.

MISS LEIGHTON. *(Into phone)* Miss Leighton at this end.—Yes.—Yes.—Very well—holding the line for thirty seconds. (1ST PAGE *enters* L.2 *with sign reading: "MR. WEISSKOPF IS ON NUMBER SIX." Shows it.)*

VAIL. Thank you so much.

FIRST PAGE. You're welcome, sir.

VAIL. Wait a minute. Now I'll give you a piece of news. I'm going to the Men's Room and if anybody wants me, I'll be in Number Three. (VAIL *exits* R.2. 1ST PAGE *exits* L.2.)

MISS LEIGHTON. *(Continuing into telephone)* Mr. Weisskopf's secretary—Miss Leighton at this end.—You will receive yesterday's equipment slips in seven minutes. Kindly have Mr. Weisskopf O.K. them. Thank you. *(Hangs up.)*

(PHYLLIS *and* FLORABEL *on from* R.1, *carrying books.)*

PHYLLIS. *(As she enters)* —by the seashore. She sells seashells by the seashore.

FLORABEL. Sixty simple supple sirens, slick and smiling, svelte and suave.

PHYLLIS. Ain't it wonderful, Miss Leighton? We can talk now.

MISS LEIGHTON. *(Rises)* Really?

FLORABEL. Yes, and a damn site better than most of them.

MISS LEIGHTON. I think your progression has been just marvelous. I can't see why they keep bringing people from New York.

FLORABEL. Yeh—people from the "legitimate" stage, whatever that is.

PHYLLIS. Yes, Miss Leighton, we've been wondering about that. What the hell *is* the legitimate stage, anyway?

MISS LEIGHTON. It's what Al Jolson used to be on before he got famous in pictures. He worked for some real estate people—the Shuberts.

FLORABEL. Do you know what someone told me at a party the other day? They said John Barrymore used to be on the legitimate stage.

PHYLLIS. I heard the same thing and I didn't believe it.

MISS LEIGHTON. My, you'd never know it from his acting, would you?

FLORABEL. And that ain't all. I heard that since John Barrymore's made good, some sister of his is trying to get out here.

MISS LEIGHTON. Oh, yes—Elsie Barrymore—— It must have been kind of interesting, the legitimate stage. Of course, it was before my time, but my grandfather used to go to it. He was in the Civil War, too.

PHYLLIS. The Civil War—— Didn't D. W. Griffith produce that?

FLORABEL. *(Crossing to door* L.2*)* Are you coming? (MAY *enters* R.I.)

PHYLLIS. Yeah——

MAY. Got a cigarette, Miss Leighton?

MISS LEIGHTON. Right here, Miss Daniels. *(Crosses to her with cigarette case.)*

PHYLLIS. Oh, Miss Daniels! I got the seashells.

FLORABEL. And I got the supple sirens.

MAY. Well, that's fine. But I won't be happy till you get the rigor mortis.

PHYLLIS. Oh, that'll be wonderful!

FLORABEL. Oh, marvelous! *(Exit* ⎫ *(Together)* FLORABEL *and* PHYLLIS L.2.) ⎭

MISS LEIGHTON. There are some people outside for the ten o'clock class, Miss Daniels. Are you ready for them? They're the stomach muscles and the abdominal breathing people.

MAY. You heard the girls' voices just now, Miss Leighton.

MISS LEIGHTON. Yes, Miss Daniels.

MAY. How did they sound to you?

MISS LEIGHTON. Oh, wonderful, Miss Daniels.

MAY. You didn't hear anything about their tests, did you? Whether Mr. Glogauer has seen 'em yet?

MISS LEIGHTON. No, I haven't. But I'm sure they'll be all right.

MAY. *(Lighting cigarette)* Thanks.

MISS LEIGHTON. Miss Daniels, I know you're very busy, but some time I'd like you to hear me in a little poem I've prepared—"Boots" by Rudyard Kipling.

MAY. *(Smiling weakly)* Fine. I've never heard "Boots" before.

MISS LEIGHTON. I've been having some trouble with the sibilant sounds, but my vowels are open, all right.

MAY. Any fever?

MISS LEIGHTON. I've tried all kinds of sibilants, but——

2ND PAGE. *(Enters L.2; takes slip to* MISS LEIGHTON*)* Miss Leighton, please.

MISS LEIGHTON. *(Not stopping)* I can't just seem to—— Excuse me. *(Her eyes sweep the note)* Oh, dear! Some of the nasal throat toners are out there with the abdominal breathers. What shall I do about it?

MAY. Tell 'em to pick out two good ones and drown the rest.

MISS LEIGHTON. How's that?

MAY. Oh, send 'em in. I'll make one job of it

MISS LEIGHTON. Yes, ma'am. *(To* 2ND PAGE*)* Understand?

PAGE. Yes, ma'am. *(Exits L.2.)*

JERRY. *(Enters* R.1 *briskly)* Say, May! *(A glance at his watch)* You've got a class waiting, haven't you?

MAY. I know.

JERRY. *(Crosses to her)* Oh, Miss Leighton—Mr. Glogauer busy? I want to see him.

MISS LEIGHTON. Afraid he is, Mr. Hyland.

JERRY. Tell him I've got some figures on the school—just take a minute.

MISS LEIGHTON. I'll tell him. But he has conference after conference all morning. In fact, at eleven fifty-seven two of his conferences overlap. I'm so ashamed. *(Exits* L.2.)

JERRY. Well, the old school is working on high, isn't it?

MAY. Jerry, are you busy for lunch?

JERRY. Afraid I am, May. Booked up pretty solid for the next two days.

MAY. Oh, I see.

JERRY. Kinda hard finding time for everything.

MAY. Isn't it, though?

JERRY. This school's a pretty big thing. You don't realize, just with the classes. But the business end keeps a fellow tied down.

MAY. Of course, Jerry. I suppose you're busy tonight?

JERRY. *(Nods)* Party up at Jack Young's.

MAY. Ah, yes. Still, I—would like to have a little chat with you—sometime.

JERRY. Why? Anything special?

MAY. We haven't really had a talk for quite a— of course, I kinda expected to see you last night—

JERRY. Oh, yes. Sorry about that, May, but I knew you'd understand. Got to trot with the right people out here. I'm meeting everybody, May. I was sorry I had to break that date with you, but—

MAY. Oh, that's all right about the date, Jerry. I

wouldn't bother you, but I do think it's kind of important.

JERRY. Why? What's happened?

MAY. Oh, nothing's happened, but—Glogauer was supposed to hear those tests last night, wasn't he?

JERRY. Sure—you mean Leigh and Fontaine?

MAY. Well, what about them? We haven't heard anything yet.

JERRY. How do you mean——? You're not nervous, are you? He just hasn't got round to it.

MAY. He was pretty anxious to get 'em—calling up all afternoon.

JERRY. Say! He's probably heard 'em already and buying up stories—that's more like it! Stop worrying, May! We haven't got a thing in the world to worry about. We're sitting pretty. (*Exit* JERRY L.2. MAY *stands looking after him a moment, then paces nervously to* L. *of the table* C. GEORGE *appears in the door* R.I, *brightly. He carries a single book, which is open.*)

GEORGE. May!

MAY. What is it?

GEORGE. Is it stomach in and chest out or stomach out and chest in or the other way around?

MAY. Huh?

GEORGE. I've got them all in there with their chests out and now I don't know what to do about it.

MAY. George, are you fooling with that class again?

GEORGE. I was just talking to them till you got ready.

MAY. Look, George. You know that big comfortable chair over in the corner for my office?

GEORGE. You mean the blue one?

MAY. That's right. Will you go and just sit in that until about February?

GEORGE. Huh?

MAY. You know, I'm only one lesson ahead of

that class myself. That's all we need yet—your fine Italian hand.

GEORGE. What do you need?

MAY. Let it go, George. *(Crosses L.)*

GEORGE. May!

MAY. *(Turning)* Yes?

GEORGE. Susan's doing all right in the school, isn't she?

MAY. Sure—great.

GEORGE. I'm awfully glad of that. She's got a new poem that would be fine for a voice test.

MAY. All right, George.

GEORGE. *(With a good deal of feeling)* "Yes, I'm a tramp—what of it? Folks say we ain't no good—"

MAY. Yes, George!

GEORGE. "Once I was strong and handsome—"

MAY. *(Comes to him)* George, will you go in—

GEORGE. She does it wonderful, May. Susan's a wonderful girl, don't you think?

MAY. Yes, George.

GEORGE. She's the kind of girl I've always been looking for, May. And she says I am, too.

MAY. George, it isn't serious between you two is it?

GEORGE. Well, Susan says she won't get married until she's carved out her career.

MAY. Oh, that's all right, then.

GEORGE. She likes me—*that* part of it's all right —but she says look at Eleanora Duse—her career almost ruined by love. Suppose I turned out to be another D'Annunzio?

MAY. She's certainly careful, that girl.

GEORGE. May, now that the school's a success, what about you?

MAY. What?

GEORGE. What about—you and Jerry?

MAY. Jerry's a busy man these days, George. We've decided to wait.

GEORGE. Oh!

MAY. Just the minute there's any news, I'll let you know.

GEORGE. Thanks, May.

MAY. Before *you* tell *me*.

GEORGE. It was a wonderful idea of Jerry's—coming out here. I guess you must be pretty proud of him.

MAY. *(Nods)* I'm working on a laurel wreath for Jerry, evenings.

GEORGE. I won't say anything about it—it'll be a surprise.

MAY. Look, George. Even when Susan has carved out her career—and I want to be there for the carving—you just do a good deal of figuring before you get married. And you come to me before you take any steps. Understand?

GEORGE. Why? I love Susan, May.

MAY. I understand, but of course all kinds of things can happen. You never can tell.

GEORGE. Can happen to Susan, you mean?

MAY. I'll tell you what might happen to Susan. She's going to be reciting "Boots" some day, and a whole crowd of people is going to start moving toward her.

GEORGE. With contracts?

MAY. Well, contracts and—— (1ST PAGE *enters* L.I.)

PAGE. There's a lady asking for Miss Susan Walker. *(Exits L.I.)*

MRS. WALKER. *(Entering on the heels of the* PAGE*)* Oh, Miss Daniels, can Susan get away for a little while? Hello, Doctor! You won't mind if Susan goes away for a little while, will you?

MAY. No, no. If you'll excuse me—— *(Starts for door* R.I.*)*

GEORGE. Is anything the matter?

MRS. WALKER. It's nothing to worry about—

Susan's father is going to call us up—long distance —down at the hotel in ten minutes—that really leaves us nine minutes. He sent a telegram and says he wants to talk to us.

GEORGE. Well, I'll get Susan. Will it be all right if I went along with you, while you telephoned?

MRS. WALKER. Why, I'd love to.

GEORGE. You don't care, do you, May?

MAY. No, indeed.

GEORGE. *(Calling)* Susan——! *(Exits* R.I.*)*

MAY. *(Again trying to leave)* I'm awfully sorry, but——

MRS. WALKER. Oh, Miss Daniels. Please don't go! I wonder if I could talk to you about Susan? I mean about how she's getting along in the school?

MAY. Of course.

MRS. WALKER. I've been kind of worried about her lately. You do think she's doing all right?

MAY. Oh, sure. I—ah—I think she's got Garbo licked a dozen ways.

MRS. WALKER. Really, Miss Daniels? What at?

MAY. Oh, pretty near everything. Crocheting—

MRS. WALKER. Oh, I'm so happy to hear you say that, because her father gets so impatient. I've tried to explain to him that it isn't so easy out here, even if you're the kind of an actress Susan is.

MAY. It's even harder if you're the kind of an actress Susan is.

MRS. WALKER. Of course. Then last week I wrote and told him what you said about her—you know—that you thought Technicolor would help? And he said for me to say to you—that you are doing the most courageous work out here since the earthquake. I couldn't understand what he was driving at.

MAY. Thanks. Just tell Mr. Walker for me that I'm doing the best I can and that the Red Cross is helping me.

MRS. WALKER. They do so much good, don't they? It's really a wonderful organization. (GEORGE *and* SUSAN *enter* R.1; *cross to door* L.1 *without pausing.)*

SUSAN. Mother, what does Father want?

GEORGE. We've got six minutes.

MRS. WALKER. I don't know, dear. My, we've got to hurry. (ALL *but* MAY *are crossing to the door* L.1.) Six minutes. Me mustn't keep Mr. Walker waiting.

GEORGE. What kind of a man is he, Mrs. Walker? Do you know him very well? (SUSAN, MRS. WALKER *and* GEORGE *exit* L.1. MAY *is up* C., *about to start for her office, when the door* R.2 *opens, and* VAIL *enters. He nods to* MAY, *and sits in his old chair.)*

MAY. Isn't there some disease you get from sitting?

VAIL. If there is, I've got it.

MAY. What do you do about meals—have them sent in?

VAIL. What's the record for these chairs—do you know?

MAY. I'm not sure—I think it was a man named Wentworth. He sat right through Hoover's administration. *(A* GIRL *peeps in at door* R.1.)

GIRL. Oh, Miss Daniels, we're waiting for you.

MAY. What?

GIRL. We're still breathing in here.

MAY. *(Rolling up a sleeve)* Yah? Well, I'll put a stop to that. *(Exits* R.1. VAIL *is alone. He rises: goes to the* C. *table and inspects a magazine. Gives it up for another, which he also glances idly through. Takes it back to his seat, drops it onto the chair and sits on it.* MISS LEIGHTON *enters* L.2. *Sees* VAIL.)

MISS LEIGHTON. Yes?

VAIL. Don't you remember me, Princess? I'm the Marathon chair sitter.

MISS LEIGHTON. What is the name, please?

VAIL. Lawrence Vail. I am waiting to see Mr. Glogauer.

MISS LEIGHTON. *(Returning to her desk)* Oh, yes. I gave him your name, but he doesn't seem to remember you. What was it about, please?

VAIL. It's about a pain in a strictly localized section.

MISS LEIGHTON. How's that?

RUDOLPH KAMMERLING. *(A German director, enters R.2. He is in a mood. He goes straight to MISS LEIGHTON)* Where is Mr. Glogauer, Miss Leighton? Get hold of him for me right away.

MISS LEIGHTON. He's on Number Eight, Mr. Kammerling.

KAMMERLING. I just come from Number Eight —he is not there.

MISS LEIGHTON. Then he must be in conference with the Exploitation people, Mr. Kammerling.

KAMMERLING. Maybe he is through. Try his office.

MISS LEIGHTON. I've just come by there. He isn't in his office.

KAMMERLING. Gott in Himmel, he must be *some* place. Try Number Eight again. (MISS LEIGHTON *takes up phone.)*

MISS LEIGHTON. Yes, Mr. Kammerling.

KAMMERLING. *(Pacing nervously up and down)* For two cents I would go back to Germany and Ufa!

MISS LEIGHTON. Number Eight. Mr. Kammerling calling Mr. Glogauer. Imperative.

KAMMERLING. *(Sees VAIL—this to him)* America! Reinhardt begged me not to come! On his knees in the Schauspielhaus he begged me! (VAIL *gives him a nod of agreement.)*

MISS LEIGHTON. Hello? Mr. Glogauer not there?

Just a moment. *(Turning)* He isn't there, Mr. Kammerling. Any message?

KAMMERLING. *(Beside himself—shouting)* Yes! Tell them I take the next boat back to Germany! Wait! Who is it on the phone?

MISS LEIGHTON. Mr. Weisskopf.

KAMMERLING. Give it to me! *(Takes the phone. MISS LEIGHTON exits L.2.)* Hello, this is Kammerling—— How much publicity is there sent out on Dorothy Dodd?—What?—We are lost!—Why? I tell you why! Because I have just seen her and she is impossible! I will not ruin my American career! *(Hangs up)* What a country—what a country! Oh, to be in Russia with Eisenstein! *(He storms out R.2.)*

(Two ELECTRICIANS enter R.I. They carry work kits.)

IST ELECTRICIAN. You take all this studio equipment—they don't know what they're getting when they buy this stuff.

2ND ELECTRICIAN. They certainly pick up a lot of junk.

IST ELECTRICIAN. Look at that baseplug—torn half way out of the socket. Socket all wrenched out of shape, too. Haven't got a new one in your bag, have you?

2ND ELECTRICIAN. Don't think so. Wait a minute. *(He looks through his tools, whistling as he does so)* No. Nothing doing.

IST ELECTRICIAN. No use till we get one—it's all torn out. *(The 2ND ELECTRICIAN, while packing up his tools, shakes his head, still whistling.)* Say, what is that? *(The 2ND ELECTRICIAN whistles a bit further—interrogatively, as if to inquire if he was referring to the melody)* Yah—is it yours? *(Still whistling, the 2ND ELECTRICIAN nods.)* Start it again. *(He does so; whistles a phrase)* I think I got the lyric. *(He improvises to the* 2ND ELECTRICIAN's *whistling)*

"By a babbling brook at twilight——
Once there sat a loving twain——"

2ND ELECTRICIAN. That's great!

1ST ELECTRICIAN. *(Hotly)* And this one doesn't go to Paramount, after the way they treated us. *(*BOTH ELECTRICIANS *exit* L.1, *singing and whistling. An* OFFICE GIRL *enters* R.1; *crosses with paper; exits* R.2. MISS LEIGHTON *enters* L.2; *starts to go down* R.; *notices* VAIL; *stops below table* C.)

MISS LEIGHTON. Yes?

VAIL. *(A long look at her before speaking)* Say it ain't true, Duchess—say you remember.

MISS LEIGHTON. Oh, yes. An appointment, wasn't it?

VAIL. That's it—an appointment. I got it through a speculator. Listen, maybe this will help. *(Rises; goes down* C.)* I work here. I have an office—a room with my name on the door. It's a big room, see? In that long hall where the authors work? The people that write? Authors! It's a room—a room with my name in gold letters on the door.

MISS LEIGHTON. What was the name again?

VAIL. Lawrence Vail.

MISS LEIGHTON. Oh, you're Lawrence *Vail*. Well, I'll tell Mr. Weisskopf—— *(Starts to go.)*

VAIL. *(Stopping her)* No, no! Just let the whole thing drop. Only tell me something—they make talking pictures here, is that right?

MISS LEIGHTON. What?

VAIL. This is a picture studio? They make pictures here—pictures that talk? They do *something* here, don't they?

MISS LEIGHTON. *(Edging away to back of desk)* I'll tell Mr. Weisskopf——

VAIL. *(Following her)* Don't be afraid of me,

little girl. I'll not harm you. It's just that I've been in that room—my office—the place with my name on the door—for months and months—nobody ever noticed me—alone in there—the strain of it—it's been too much. And so I came out. *(He barks it out. MISS LEIGHTON jumps back.)* I don't expect to see Mr. Glogauer any more—I just want to go in and wander around. Because tomorrow I'm going home, and I want to tell them I saw 'em made. Who knows —maybe I'll run into Mr. Glogauer—I'd love to know what God looks like before I die. *(Exits L.2.)*

MISS LEIGHTON. Yes—yes—I'll tell Mr. Weiss-kopf. *(Sinks into desk chair.)*

HELEN. *(Entering L.1)* Good morning, Miss Leighton!

MISS LEIGHTON. *(Weakly)* Good morning.

HELEN. My dear, what *is* the matter? You're shaking.

MISS LEIGHTON. There was a drunken man in here just now.

HELEN. You poor child. Well, they'll soon be weeded out—Will Hays is working as fast as he can.

MISS LEIGHTON. Yes, I know.

HELEN. Dorothy Dodd get here, Miss Leighton?

MISS LEIGHTON. Yes, she got in this morning.

HELEN. They say she's simply gorgeous. I do want to meet her. You know, more people have told me I look like her. *(Crossing to table C.)* Tell me, Miss Leighton. My paper wants me to try to find— *(Delving into bag)* What *is* his name? He works here. *(Finds slip of paper)* Lawrence Vail.

MISS LEIGHTON. Lawrence Vail? No, I don't think I ever heard of him. *(Rises)* Is he a director?

HELEN. No, no, he's a playwright. From New York. He's supposed to have come out here a long time ago and nothing's been heard of him . He seems to have just disappeared.

MISS LEIGHTON. Why, isn't that terrible. Have you tried Paramount?

HELEN. No, he's not at Paramount. They've lost six playwrights of their own in the past month. Once they get out of their rooms, nobody knows what becomes of them. You'd think they'd lock the doors, wouldn't you?

MISS LEIGHTON. *(Going to her desk and taking a stack of cards from a drawer)* Yes—that's what we do. *(Looking through cards)* Lawrence Vail. I'm sure he isn't one of our playwrights, because if he was I'd be sure to—— *(Finds the card she is seeking)* Well, isn't that strange? *(Bringing out card)* He *is* one of our playwrights. *(Reads)* "Lawrence Vail."

HELEN. *(Looking over her shoulder)* That's the man.

MISS LEIGHTON. *(Eyes on card)* Yes—he came out here on October eighteenth. From New York City. He was one of a shipment of sixteen playwrights.

HELEN. *(Reading)* "Dark hair, brown eyes——"

MAY. *(Entering R.1)* Oh, hello, Helen.

HELEN. *(With no warmth whatever)* May, dear.

MISS LEIGHTON. Suppose I look in the playwrights' room. Maybe he's there.

HELEN. Oh, thanks, Miss Leighton. Shall I come along with you?

MISS LEIGHTON. No, if he's there I'll find him. Though I sort of hate to go down where they keep the playwrights—it always scares me—those padded walls and the bars over the windows. *(Exits L.2.)*

HELEN. *(Looking at her watch, starts for the door L.1)* My, nearly twelve o'clock! I'd no idea!

MAY. Oh, must you go? You're quite a stranger these days.

HELEN. Yes—the mad, mad pace of Hollywood!
I have two luncheons to go to—the Timken Ball
Bearing people are having a convention here and it's
also the fifth anniversary of Golden Bear Cookies.

MAY. Well, if you have just a minute I'd like
to——

HELEN. The Cookie people are so prompt——

MAY. I just wondered how you thought everything was going, Helen.

HELEN. Oh, wonderful, wonderful! You know,
my column is being translated into Spanish now—
they'll be reading it way over in Moscow.

MAY. Yes, that's fine. But what I was going to
ask you was—have you heard anything about the
school lately? How everybody thinks it's going.

HELEN. *(Evasively)* Well, of course you'd know
more than I do about that—after all, it's *your* en-
terprise. Naturally I'd be the last person to——

MAY. Then you *have* heard something, haven't
you, Helen? Who from—Glogauer?

HELEN. *(Turns to* MAY*)* Why, of course not,
May—whatever gave you such an idea? Of course
you never can tell about things out here—sometimes
something will just happen to catch on, and then
again—*well!* *(The final "Well!" is a sort of grand
dismissal of the subject, coupled with relief at having got that far. She is on the verge of departure.)*

MAY. *(With quiet dignity)* Thanks, Helen. I'm
very grateful.

HELEN. Well, I—ah—— *(Turning to her)* I
don't imagine you've made any plans for the future?

MAY. Not yet.

HELEN. After all, I suppose you've got all of
your friends in England—it's only natural that——

MAY. Oh, yes. All of them.

HELEN. Well, I may be coming over in the spring
—and if I do we must get together.

MAY. By all means.

HELEN. Well! *(She beams on her)* Bon voyage!
*(She goes out L.I. MAY stands looking after her,
then starts for the door R.I. The R.2 door opens. A
gentleman named MR. FLICK, carrying various
strange boxes, looms in the doorway.)*

FLICK. Pardon me, but can you tell me where I
am?

MAY. What?

FLICK. Do you know where I am? I'm looking
for the office of—— *(Takes out paper. Reading)*
Miss May Daniels, Mr. Jerome Hyland, Dr. George
Lewis.

MAY. I'm Miss Daniels. What do you want?

FLICK. Oh, I don't want you. I just want to know
where your office is.

MAY. *(A gesture to R.I)* Right through there.

FLICK. Thanks. *(Starts.)*

MAY. You won't find anybody in there.

FLICK. Oh, that's all right. I've only got to do
some work on the door.

MAY. Oh! On the door?

FLICK. I just gotta take the names off.

MAY. You mean Daniels, Hyland and Lewis are
coming off the door?

FLICK. That's right.

MAY. So that's your business, is it—taking names
off doors?

FLICK. No, I put 'em on too. I do more door
work than anybody else in Hollywood. Out at First
National the other day I went right through the studio—every door. Why, some of the peope didn't
even know they were out till they saw me taking
their names off.

MAY. Must have been a nice surprise.

FLICK. Yes, sometimes they leave their office and
go out to lunch and by the time they get back it
says, "Barber Shop."

MAY. We aren't even out to lunch.

FLICK. Well, if you'll excuse me——

MAY. Yes, you've got your work to do. Well, it's been very nice to have met you.

FLICK. Much obliged.

MAY. *(Opening the* R.I *door for him)* You're sure you know where it is? Right at the end of the corridor—see?

FLICK. *(Looking off)* Oh, yes. Miss May Daniels, Mr. Jerome Hyland—— *(Exit* R.I. MAY *stands at the door for a moment.* MISS CHASEN *enters* R.2; *crosses; exits* L.I. MAY *walks slowly toward* L.C. JERRY *enters* L.2 *as* CHASEN *exits—briskly whistling. Crosses to down* R.C.)

MAY. *(Quietly)* Say, Jerry.

JERRY. Huh?

MAY. Have you got a minute?

JERRY. Gosh, May—afraid I haven't.

MAY. Yes, you have.

JERRY. I've got to see Weisskopf right away.

MAY. No, you don't.

JERRY. What?

MAY. You don't have to see Weisskopf.

JERRY. Yah, but I do.

MAY. No, you don't.

JERRY. What are you talking about?

MAY. *(Very lightly)* Did you ever hear the story of the three bears?

JERRY. Huh!

MAY. There was the Papa Bear, and the Mama Bear, and the Camembert. They came out to Hollywood to start a voice school—remember? A couple of them were engaged to be married or something—that's right, they were engaged—whatever happened to that?

JERRY. Wha-at?

MAY. Well, anyway, they *did* start a voice school —What do you think of that? They started a voice

school, and had a big office, and everything was lovely. And then suddenly they came to work one morning, and where their office had been there was a beautiful fountain instead. And the Mama Bear said to the
Papa Bear, "What the hell do you know about that?"

JERRY. May, stop clowning! What is it?

MAY. And this came as a great big surprise to
the Papa Bear, because *he* thought that everything
that glittered just *had* to be gold.

JERRY. Say, if you're going to talk in circles——

MAY. All right—I'll stop talking in circles. We're
washed up, Jerry.

JERRY. What are you talking about?

MAY. I said we're washed up. Through, finished,
and out!

JERRY. What do you mean we're out? Why—who
said we were out?

MAY. I knew it myself when we didn't hear about
those tests—I felt it. And then ten minutes ago
Helen Hobart walked in here.

JERRY. What did she say?

MAY. She handed the school right back to us—it
seems she had nothing to do with it. That tells the
story.

JERRY. That doesn't mean anything. You can't
tell from what she says.

MAY. Oh, you can't, eh? Then I'll show you
something that does mean something—(GEORGE *enters* L.1) —and see if you can answer this one!

GEORGE. *(In a state of high excitement)* May!
May, something terrible has happened!

MAY. I know it!

GEORGE. You can't! It's Mr. Walker! Susan has
to go back home—they're leaving tomorrow!

JERRY. May, what were you starting
to tell me?

GEORGE. Did you hear what I said,
May?

} *(Together)*

JERRY. Shut up, George! *(To* MAY*)*
What were you going to tell me?
GEORGE. Susan has got to go back
home!

} *(Together)*

MAY. *(Breaking in)* For God's sake, stop a minute! George, we've got more important things!

GEORGE. There couldn't be more important things!
JERRY. *(At* GEORGE's *interruption)*
Oh, for the love of——

} *(Together)*

MAY. Well, there are! We're fired, George—we haven't got jobs any more!

GEORGE. What?
JERRY. How do you know, May?
How do you know we're fired?

} *(Together)*

MAY. I'll show you how I know! *(She goes to the door* R.I *and opens it. In a trance they follow her and look off.)*

JERRY. *(In a hushed tone)* Gosh!

GEORGE. You mean the window washer?

JERRY. *(Stunned)* Why—why, I was talking to Glogauer only yesterday——

MAY. Well, there you are, Jerry. So you see it's true.

GEORGE. You mean—you mean there isn't any school any more?

MAY. That's the idea, George.

GEORGE. But—but—why? Then—what about Susan?

MAY. Oh, let up on Susan! Besides, I thought you said she was going home.

GEORGE. Yah, but if we could get her a job right away! (MAY, *with a look, turns away from him.* MR. FLICK *enters* R.I *with scraper and tool-kit in hand. Crosses cheerfully, with a nod to* ALL.)

MAY. Well, that was quick work.

FLICK. Oh, it don't take long. You see, on those doors I never use permanent paint. *(Exits* L.2 *with-*

out having paused in his cross. A pause after his departure.)

MAY. Well, I suppose we might as well get our things together. *(She starts to cross; looks at the disconsolate figure of* JERRY*)* Don't take it so hard, Jerry. We've been up against it before.

JERRY. But everything was so—— I don't know which way to turn, May. It's kind of knocked me all of a heap.

MAY. Don't let it lick you, Jerry—we'll pull out of it some way. We always have.

JERRY. Yah, but—not this. A thing like this sort of—— What are we going to do?

MAY. What do you say we go to Hollywood? I hear they're panicstricken out there. They'll fall on the necks of the first people—— *(Exit* JERRY *and* MAY R.I. GEORGE *is alone.* METERSTEIN *and* WEISS-KOPF *enter* L.I *and cross to exit* R.2.*)*

WEISSKOPF. But the important thing is your retakes.

METERSTEIN. That's it—your retakes.

WEISSKOPF. You take your retakes—— *(*SUSAN *enters* L.I.*)* —and if they aren't good you've got no picture.

METERSTEIN. Oh, it's the retakes. ⎫
WEISSKOPF. Yah, it's the retakes, ⎪
all right. *(They exit* R.2.*)* ⎪
GEORGE. *(Eagerly)* Susan! Any- ⎬ *(Together)*
thing happen? After I left? ⎪
SUSAN. *(Forlornly)* I just came ⎪
back to get my books and things. *(In* ⎪
his arms) Oh, George! ⎭

GEORGE. *(His arms around her)* Susan, you can't go back like this—it isn't fair! Why, you were just made for the talkies—you and I both! Did you tell your father we were waiting for Technicolor?

SUSAN. *(Crossing)* He just said stop being a goddam fool and come on home.

GEORGE. But giving up with your career only half carved!

SUSAN. He wants Mother home, too. He says eating all his meals in restaurants, that it's ruining his stomach.

GEORGE. But you've got your own life to live—you can't give up your career on account of your father's stomach!

SUSAN. It's no use, George. You don't know Father. Why, when the first talking picture came to Columbus he stood up and talked right back to it.

GEORGE. I guess your father's a pretty hard man to get on with.

SUSAN. Oh, you don't know, George. It's going to be terrible, going back to Columbus, after all this.

GEORGE. I'm not going to let you go back, Susan. Something's got to be done about it.

SUSAN. But it's so hopeless, George. (SUSAN *exits* R.I. GEORGE *stands a moment, puzzled, slaps his hand with his fist.* MISS LEIGHTON *enters* L.2, *crosses down to her desk, still carrying the* LAWRENCE VAIL *card.)*

GEORGE. Could you find Mr. Glogauer for me?

MISS LEIGHTON. Sorry, Doctor—I'm terribly worried. I'm looking for a playwright, and there's a drunken man following me all around. (MISS LEIGHTON *exits* L.I.)

(LAWRENCE VAIL *enters* L.2 *as* LEIGHTON *goes through the other door; goes to chair for his coat.* GEORGE *watches him as he brings his magazine back to the table.)*

GEORGE. Excuse me, but have you seen Mr. Glogauer? (VAIL, *his eyes on* GEORGE, *drops the magazine onto the table; goes back to the chair for his hat.)* I've been trying to find him, but nobody knows where he is.

VAIL. You one of the chosen people?

GEORGE. *(Insulted)* What?

VAIL. Do you work here?

GEORGE. Oh! I thought you meant was I—yah. I'm Doctor Lewis.

VAIL. Oh, yes. About Mr. Glogauer. *(Putting on coat)* Tell me something—it won't go any further. Have you ever seen Mr. Glogauer?

GEORGE. Oh, yes. Lots of times.

VAIL. Actually seen him, huh? I suppose you've been here a good many years. *(Gets hat.)*

GEORGE. *(Shakes head)* No. Only about six weeks.

VAIL. Only six weeks. I wouldn't have thought it possible.

GEORGE. Do you work here too?

VAIL. Yes. Yes. You see, Doctor, I'm supposed to be a playwright. Probably it doesn't mean anything to you, but my name is Lawrence Vail. (GEORGE'S *face is a complete blank.)* It *doesn't* mean anything to you, does it?

GEORGE. No.

VAIL. *(Crossing* R.*)* No, I wouldn't have thought so.

GEORGE. Well, is that what you're doing here—writing plays?

VAIL. Not so far I'm not.

GEORGE. Well, then, what are you doing?

VAIL. *(Sadly)* Don't ask me that. I don't know. I don't know anything about it. I didn't want to come out to this god-forsaken country. I have a beautiful apartment in New York—and friends. But they hounded me, and hammered at me and belabored me, till you would have thought if I didn't get out here by the fifteenth of October every camera in Hollywood would stop clicking.

GEORGE. You don't say?

VAIL. And so I came. In a moment of weakness I came. That was six months ago. I have an office, and a secretary, and I draw my salary every week, but so far no one has taken the slightest notice of me. I haven't received an assignment, I haven't met anybody outside of the girl who hands me my check. In short, Doctor Lewis, I haven't done a single thing.

GEORGE. Why do you suppose they were so anxious to have you come out, then?

VAIL. Who knows? Why do you suppose they have these pages dressed the way they are, and those signs, and that woman at the desk, or this room, or a thousand other things?

GEORGE. Don't you like it out here?

VAIL. *(An unbelieving look at* GEORGE *first)* Doctor Lewis, I think Hollywood and this darling industry of yours is the most God-awful thing I've ever run into. Everybody behaving in the most fantastic fashion—nobody acting like a human being. I'm brought out here, like a hundred others, paid a fat salary—nobody notices me. Not that I might be any good—it's just an indication. Thousands of dollars thrown away every day. Why do they do that, do you know?

GEORGE. No, sir.

VAIL. There you are. Plenty of good minds have come out here. Why aren't they used? Why must everything be dressed up in this hokum—waiting in a room like this, and having those morons thrust a placard under your nose every minute. Why is that?

GEORGE. I don't know.

VAIL. Me neither. The whole business is in the hands of incompetents, that's all. But I don't have to *stay* here, and I'm not going to. I've tried to see Mr. Glogauer—God knows I've tried to see him. But it can't be done. So just tell him for me that he can take his contract and put it where it will do the most good. I'm going home, and thank you very much for listening to me. *(He has crossed* GEORGE *and is at the door* L.I.)

GEORGE. There's a lot in what you say, Mr. Vail. I've been having a good deal of trouble myself.

VAIL. You bet there's a lot in what I say. Only somebody ought to tell it to Glogauer.

GEORGE. That's right. Well, look—why don't you make an appointment with Mr. Glogauer and tell him?

VAIL. *(Raising his hand in a farewell)* Goodbye, Doctor—— *(It is too much for* VAIL. *He exits* L.I.)

GEORGE. (GEORGE *is alone. He thinks it over, then decides that action of some sort has to be taken. He goes to the telephone)* Hello—— This is Doctor Lewis—Doctor Lewis—— Well, I work here. That is, I—ah—I've got to get in touch with Mr. Glogauer. (GLOGAUER *and* KAMMERLING *enter* R.I *in the middle of a hot argument.* GEORGE, *of course, hangs up the receiver immediately.)*

GLOGAUER. What can I do about it now? Miss Leighton! Where is Miss Leighton? You know just how we are fixed. What can I do about it at a time like this? You know just who we've got available. What do you want me to do about it?

GEORGE. Oh! Mr. Glogauer!

KAMMERLING. No, no, no! There is no use of going on! Dorothy Dodd will not do! I will go back to Germany and Ufa before I shoot a foot!

GEORGE. Mr. Glogauer, could I talk to you for a minute?

KAMMERLING. She is not the type!

(Together)

She is not what I want! You have⎤
only got to look at her! |
  GLOGAUER. *(Into the phone)* Get |
Miss Leighton for me—right away. ⎬ *(Together)*
  KAMMERLING.   The   minute   she |
walked into the studio. |
  GEORGE. Mr. Glogauer——   ⎦
  GLOGAUER. *(Finally outshouting* KAMMERLING*)*
Do you realize that I brought that woman from New
York, took her out of a show, and she's on a play
or pay contract for the next three months? Besides
she's got a big legit name! Take her out, he says!
(GEORGE, *a little bowled over by the momentum of
all this, is above the table* C., *with* GLOGAUER L. *and*
KAMMERLING R., *between the two fires, and pretty
bewildered by it all.)*

  KAMMERLING. But I will not have my work
ruined! She will be terrible—she is not the type!

  GLOGAUER. Then go to work on her! What are
you a director for?

  KAMMERLING. No, no—she is a good actress, but
it is the wrong part. The part is a country girl—a
girl from the country!

  GLOGAUER. Don't I know that?

  KAMMERLING. But Dorothy Dodd is not a country girl. She is a woman—a woman who has lived
with a dozen men—and looks it! Can I make her
over? I am just a director—not God!

  GLOGAUER. But if it was explained to her! How
long would it take to explain a country girl?

  KAMMERLING. But everyone knows about her—
it's been in the newspapers—every time they break
a door down they find *her.*

  GLOGAUER. But what am I to do at a time like
this?

  KAMMERLING. Get somebody else! Somebody
that looks it!

  GEORGE. Mr. Glogauer——

KAMMERLING. *(Not stopping)* My direction would go for nothing! My work would be ruined!

GLOGAUER. Let me get this straight—— You mean she *positively* won't do?

KAMMERLING. *Positively.*

GLOGAUER. Well, if it's posi*tive*ly I suppose there's nothing for it.

KAMMERLING. Ah!

GLOGAUER. *(Not stopping)* We got to get somebody, then, and quick!

KAMMERLING. Now you're again the artist. Somebody like Janet Gaynor—she would be fine. Maybe Fox would lend her to you.

GEORGE. *(Weakly)* I know who could do it.

GLOGAUER. *(Speaking over GEORGE)* Maybe Warners would lend me John Barrymore! Don't talk foolish, Kammerling. I went over our list of people with you and you know just who we've got available.

GEORGE. *(Stronger this time)* I know somebody could do it.

GLOGAUER. *(Not stopping)* I can't do a magician act—take somebody out of my pocket. You know just who we got!

GEORGE. *(Making himself heard)* But I know exactly the person.

GLOGAUER. You what?

GEORGE. *(Excited)* I know an actress who would fit the part perfectly.

KAMMERLING. Who?
GLOGAUER. What's her name? Who } *(Together)*
is she?

GEORGE. Her name is Susan Walker.

KAMMERLING. Who?
GLOGAUER. I never heard of her. } *(Together)*
What's she done?

GEORGE. She hasn't done anything.

GLOGAUER. Hasn't done anything! Taking up

our time with a girl—we must have a name! **Don't**
you understand? We must have a name!

GEORGE. Why?

GLOGAUER. What's that?

GEORGE. Why must you have a name?

GLOGAUER. Why must we have—— Go away! **Go**
away! Why must we have a name? I spend three
hundred thousand dollars on a picture and he **asks**
me—because Susan Walker as a name wouldn't draw
flies—that's why! Not flies!

GEORGE. But she could play the part.

GLOGAUER. So what? Who would come to see
her? Why do you argue on such a foolish subject?
Everybody knows you can't do a picture without a
name. What are you talking about?

GEORGE. *(Very determinedly)* Mr. Glogauer,
there's something you ought to know.

GLOGAUER. What?

GEORGE. *(Trying to remember it)* This darling
industry of yours is the most God-awful thing I've
ever run into.

GLOGAUER. What's that? *(Stares at him.)*

GEORGE. *(Gathering momentum)* Why don't people act human, anyhow? Why are you so fantastic?
Why do you go and bring all these people out here,
whoever they are, and give them all this money, and
then you don't do anything about it. Thousands of
dollars—right under your nose. Why is that?

GLOGAUER. Huh?

GEORGE. *(He realizes that that is not exactly
right)* Can you tell me why in the world you can't
make pictures without having the stars playing parts
they don't fit, just because she's got a good name
or something? How about a girl that *hasn't* got a
good name? And how about all these signs, and
this room, and that girl, and everything? And
everything else? It's the most God-awful—— *(Re-
membering some more)* All kinds of people have

come out here—why don't you do something about it? Why don't you do something about a person like Miss Walker, and give her a chance? Why, she'd be wonderful! The whole business is in the hands of incompetents, that's what's the trouble! Afraid to give anybody a chance! And you turned the Vitaphone down! (GLOGAUER *gives him a startled look.*) Yes, you did! They're all afraid to tell it to you! That's what's the matter with this business. It's in the hands of—— *(The final accusation)* —you turned the Vitaphone down! *(He turns away; cracks a couple of Indian nuts, quite satisfied with himself.)*

GLOGAUER. *(Stunned; slowly thinking it over)* By God, he's right!

GEORGE. *(Not expecting this)* Huh?

GLOGAUER. He's right! And to stand up there and tell me that—that's colossal!

GEORGE. You mean what *I* said?

GLOGAUER. That's what we need in this business —a man who can come into it, and when he sees mistakes being made, talk out about them. Yes, sir— it's colossal.

GEORGE. *(If it's as easy as that)* Why, it's the most God-awful thing—that I ever——

KAMMERLING. Who is this man? Where did he come from?

GLOGAUER. Yes, who are you? Didn't I sign you up or something?

GEORGE. I'm Doctor Lewis.

GLOGAUER. Who?

GEORGE. You know—the school.

GLOGAUER. The school? But that school isn't any good.

GEORGE. *(Moved to an accidental assertiveness)* It *is* good!

GLOGAUER. Is it?

GEORGE. *(With sudden realization that an emphatic manner can carry the day)* Why, of course it is. You people go around here turning things down—doing this and doing that——

GLOGAUER. *(To* KAMMERLING*)* He's right! Look—I pretty near fired him! I *did* fire him.

GEORGE. You see? And here's Susan Walker—just made for the talkies.

GLOGAUER. Say, who is this girl?

KAMMERLING. Where is she?⎱ *(Together)*
GLOGAUER. Tell us about her.⎰

GEORGE. Well—Mr. Kammerling knows her—I introduced her.

GLOGAUER. She's here in Hollywood?

GEORGE. Oh, sure! She just went——

KAMMERLING. I remember! She might be able to do it! She is dumb enough.

GEORGE. Shall I bring her in?

GLOGAUER. Yes, yes—let's see her!

GEORGE. She's right out here. *(Exits* R.I.*)*

GLOGAUER. Fine, fine! We'll take a look at her. There is a big man, Kammerling! I can tell! Suddenly it comes out—that's the way it always is!

KAMMERLING. In Germany, too!

GLOGAUER. Turned the Vitaphone down—no one ever dared say that to me! I got to hang on to this fellow—take options. (MISS LEIGHTON *enters* L.I.)

MISS LEIGHTON. Did you send for me, Mr. Glogauer?

GLOGAUER. Yes! Where's my coffee? I want my coffee!

MISS LEIGHTON. Yes, Mr. Glogauer—where will you have it?

GLOGAUER. Where will I have it? Where *am* I? Answer me that! Where am I?

MISS LEIGHTON. Why—right here, Mr. Glogauer.

GLOGAUER. All right—then that's where I want my coffee.

MISS LEIGHTON. Yes, sir.

GLOGAUER. And tell Meterstein I want him—**right away**. And Miss Chasen, with her notebook.

MISS LEIGHTON. Yes, sir. *(Exits* L.I.*)*

GLOGAUER. Now I show you how we handle this! We'll have *her* and a name too! We'll create a name for her! I've done it before and I do it again!

GEORGE. *(Rushes in with* SUSAN*)* Here she is, Mr. Glogauer—here she is!

KAMMERLING. If only she looks like it——

GLOGAUER. Yes! Yes! She can do it! He's right!

KAMMERLING. Ya, ya! Wunderbar!

(Together)

GEORGE. Of course I'm right.

KAMMERLING. Say "I love you."

SUSAN. "I love you."

KAMMERLING. "I hate you."

SUSAN. *(In exactly the same tone as before)* "I hate you."

KAMMERLING. She can do it!
GLOGAUER. That's wonderful!   *(Together)*

GEORGE. Sure it is!

GLOGAUER. No time to talk salary now, Miss Walker—(MISS CHASEN *enters* L.I) —but you don't have to worry!

MISS CHASEN. Yes, Mr. Glogauer!

SUSAN. Oh, George!

GEORGE. Susan!

GLOGAUER. *(Speaking on* MISS CHASEN'S *entrance)* Ah, Miss Chasen! Where's Meterstein? I want Meterstein.

METERSTEIN. *(Enters* L.2*)* Here I am, Mr. Glogauer.

GLOGAUER. Listen to this, Meterstein! Miss

Chasen, take this down. Tell the office to drop everything they're doing and concentrate on this. Drop everything, no matter what it is.

MISS CHASEN. *(Over her notes)* Drop everything.

GLOGAUER. Wire the New York office that Susan Walker, a new English actress we've just signed, will arrive in New York next week—— *(A quick aside to* GEORGE*)* I want her to go to New York first.

GEORGE. Yes, sir.

SUSAN. Does he mean me?

KAMMERLING. Yes, yes!

GLOGAUER. *(Not stopping)* Have them arrange a reception at the Savoy-Plaza—get her picture in every paper. Tell them I want her photographed with Grover Whalen.

METERSTEIN. Grover Whalen.

GLOGAUER. I want everybody in the studio to get busy on this right away. Everybody! And get hold of Davis for me right away.

MISS CHASEN. Get Davis!

METERSTEIN. *(Calling out the* L.2 *door)* Get Davis!

VOICE. *(Off)* Get Davis!

VOICE. *(Further off)* Get Davis!

GLOGAUER. Get hold of *"Photoplay"* and *"Motion Picture Magazine"* and the trade papers—I want them all. Send for Helen Hobart and tell her I want to see her personally. And I want Baker to handle this—not Davis. Never mind Davis!

METERSTEIN. Never mind Davis!

VOICE. *(Off)* Never mind Davis!

VOICE. *(Further off)* Never mind Davis!

GLOGAUER. I want national publicity on this—outdoor advertising, twenty-four sheets, everything! Meterstein, arrange a conference for me with the whole Publicity Department this afternoon. That's all.

METERSTEIN. Yes, sir. *(Goes off L.2.)*

SUSAN. Oh, George! What'll Father say now?

GLOGAUER. *(Not stopping)* Miss Chasen, shoot those wires right off!

MISS CHASEN. *(Rising)* Yes, sir.

GLOGAUER. *(Not stopping)* I'll be in my office in ten minutes, and no appointments for me for the rest of the day. That clear?

MISS CHASEN. Yes, sir. *(Exit L.I.)*
GLOGAUER. Now, then, Doctor, tear up your old contract! } *(Together)*

GEORGE. I haven't got one!

GLOGAUER. You are in charge of this whole thing —understand? What you say goes!

GEORGE. Yes, sir.

SUSAN. George, does that mean——

GLOGAUER. *(Not stopping)* When I have faith in a man the sky's the limit! You know what I do with you, Doctor? I make you supervisor in full charge—over all productions of the Glogauer Studio!

GEORGE. All right. *(Very matter-of-factly.* MAY *and* JERRY *enter* R.I. JERRY *carrying a brief case,* MAY *with her hat on,* BOTH *obviously ready to leave.)* May! Jerry! What do you think? I've just been made supervisor!

SUSAN. Yes!
JERRY. Huh!   } *(Together)*
MAY. What!

GEORGE. I told him about the Vitaphone!

(WARN Curtain.)

MAY. You what?

GLOGAUER. The one man! *(To* GEORGE*)* Tomorrow morning you get your office—with a full staff!

GEORGE. *(To* MAY *and* JERRY*)* Hear that?

ACT THREE

SCENE I

A set on the GLOGAUER *lot.*

The Curtain rises on a scene of rather vague activity. Up Right is a church altar, set against a background of church wall and stained glass window. Up Left is another piece of church wall, and in front of it a couple of church pews. Between these two pieces, and at their Right and Left, are pieces of monk's cloth, hung to deaden sound, and parts of various unrelated scenery that will presently turn into ships, railway stations, and the like. There are two studio chairs grouped just about at Center, and a few other chairs dotted here and there at the sides. Two huge cameras, one on a tripod, the other on a truck, are at the Left—the tripod camera upstage, the other downstage. In the nature of things there are three spots from which people can come on—Left, Right, and upstage C. between the two church pieces.

From offstage, at the rise, comes a busy sound of SAWING, followed by the HAMMERING in of nails. The IST LIGHT MAN *is at a light that just peeps over the Right church wall, back of the altar. The* 2ND LIGHT MAN *and* IST CAMERMAN *are at the altar, trying lights and*

89

giving instructions about their focusing. In one pew sits the 1ST BRIDESMAID, *in another the* BISHOP, *busy with a newspaper.* 2ND *and* 3D BRIDESMAIDS *are in the two downstage chairs, at Center.* 2D CAMERMAN *is at the upstage camera, and the* TRUCKMAN *on the truck that carries the first camera. There is a hanging microphone on a boom, so set that it can swing all the way over the altar.*

It is the last day of shooting on SUSAN WAL-KER'S *picture, "Gingham and Orchids," and the scene is nothing more than the usual getting set of cameras and lights, the usual yelling and the usual standing about, the inevitable waiting that is part and parcel of the whole business of taking pictures.*

2ND BRIDESMAID. *(Rising)* Get your legs out of the way, will you?

3RD BRIDESMAID. Where are you going?

2ND BRIDESMAID. Oh, I don't know—get a soda.

3RD BRIDESMAID. You just had one.

2ND BRIDESMAID. No use sitting around here. *(Exits up* L.*)*

4TH BRIDESMAID. *(Enters from* R.1*)* Say, I hear Paramount sent a call out.

1ST BRIDESMAID. What for?

4TH BRIDESMAID. Some picture without Buddy Rogers.

1ST CAMERAMAN. Hey, Les! Have you got this straight?

TRUCKMAN. Got what?

1ST CAMERAMAN. This truck shot—the finish of the ceremony.

TRUCKMAN. What ceremony?

1ST CAMERAMAN. The one they began yesterday—they're going to take the finish of it.

TRUCKMAN. I thought they took it.

1ST CAMERAMAN. Well, they didn't. When I give you the arm you roll her up—that's all you've got to remember.

3RD BRIDESMAID. I'll bet there's a catch in it somewhere.

5TH BRIDESMAID. *(Enters up* L., *crossing to sit in first pew)* Say, Dot, what are you going to do tonight?

4TH BRIDESMAID. We're going to be right here.

1ST BRIDESMAID. Don't say that! I've got big plans.

4TH BRIDESMAID. Well, you can roll them up in camphor. I know the way these last days are.

1ST ELECTRICIAN. *(Appearing* C.*)* Hey, Butch! Butch!

2ND ELECTRICIAN. *(Off* L.*)* Yah?

1ST ELECTRICIAN. Gotta fix this mike over on Thirty-one!

2ND ELECTRICIAN. *(Entering up* L.*)* Okay! Right with you!

1ST ELECTRICIAN. New mike over on Thirty-one.

(GEORGE'S SECRETARY enters up L. *on a busy tour of inspection; crosses; exits* R.1.*)*

TRUCKMAN. They going to do this now?

1ST CAMERAMAN. That's what they said when they chopped off yesterday.

TRUCKMAN. Well, I'm ready.

2ND LIGHT MAN. Hey, Weber!

2ND CAMERAMAN. Yah?

2ND LIGHT MAN. *(Walking around)* When do you lose me?

2ND CAMERAMAN. *(Peering through camera)* Now!

2ND LIGHT MAN. Do you get the Bishop? He's up here!

2ND CAMERAMAN. I don't catch the Bishop. I stay on the bride and groom.

1ST CAMERAMAN. You gotta catch him. I pick up the bride and groom.

1ST PAGE. Mr. Meterstein! Paging Mr. Meterstein!

BISHOP. Oh, boy!

(The offstage SAWING and HAMMERING stop.)

PAGE. Yes, sir.

2ND ELECTRICIAN. Have we got time?

1ST ELECTRICIAN. Sure. We ain't going anywheres. (ELECTRICIANS *exit up* C. BISHOP *crosses to down* C.)

2ND CAMERAMAN. Gotta soften those lights!

2ND LIGHT MAN. Hey! Grits! Soften 'em!

(1ST PAGE *enters* R.I.)

1ST LIGHT MAN. *(From on high)* Right!

2ND LIGHT MAN. Use your inkies.

1ST LIGHT MAN. Right!

1ST ELECTRICIAN. *(Entering up* C.) Hey, Jimmy, as soon as we knock off here we're going down to twenty-eight. *(Exit up* C.)

LEADING MAN. *(Enters* R.I) Anything doing yet?

4TH BRIDESMAID. Don't talk silly.

1ST BRIDESMAID. Just don't talk.

LEADING MAN. I'm going down to the cafeteria, if anything starts. *(Exits* R.I.)

BISHOP. *(This speech to be heard by itself)* Can you go out and get me a copy of *"Racing Form"?* Here you are. *(Hands him a dime.)*

PAGE. I'll try.

1ST LIGHT MAN. Hey, Spike!

BISHOP. Yah?

1ST LIGHT MAN. What are you playing?

BISHOP. I've got one in the fourth at Caliente, looks good. Princess Fanny.

1ST LIGHT MAN. Whose?

BISHOP. *(Going back to pew)* Princess Fanny.

2ND LIGHT MAN. Miss Walker stands here, Les. Do you get her?

TRUCKMAN. Shift her just a little bit.

1ST CAMERAMAN. Shift her is right!

2ND LIGHT MAN. Now, how's that?

2ND CAMERAMAN. Looks better.

(6TH BRIDESMAID *enters from up* L.)

6TH BRIDESMAID. Where the hell is the Bishop? *(Sees him)* Oh, there you are! *(Sits chair* R.C.*)*

4TH BRIDESMAID. Well, I hereby resign. *(Exit* R.I.*)*

2ND LIGHT MAN. *(To the* IST LIGHT MAN*)* All right—let it go at that.

IST LIGHT MAN. All right.

BISHOP. *(Sitting down again in second pew)* You know, these pews are damned comfortable. I should have gone to church long ago.

2ND CAMERAMAN. *(Through his camera)* Yah, that's it.

BISHOP. Well, good-night.

6TH BRIDESMAID. Good-night.

BISHOP. There's nothing like a good Simmons pew.

(IST ELECTRICIAN *appears up* C. GEORGE'S SECRE-
    TARY *enters* R.I, *whistling, crosses, and exits up*
    L. *Offstage SAWING resumes.*)

IST ELECTRICIAN. Hey, Mixer! Mixer!

MIXER. *(Offstage)* What do you want?

IST ELECTRICIAN. How are we on sound?

(MRS. WALKER *enters* R.I *and begins speaking.*)

MIXER. O. K. *(The SAWING offstage ceases.)*

MRS. WALKER. *(To the* BRIDESMAIDS, *sitting* C.*)* Well, I've just had the most exciting news. Susan's father is coming on for the wedding. Isn't that just too lovely?

6TH BRIDESMAID. I'm all choked up inside. (2ND ELECTRICIAN *enters up* C.; *crosses; exits up* L.)

MRS. WALKER. He wasn't coming at first—it

looked as if he'd have to go to Bermuda with the Elks. You know the Elks are in Bermuda.

6TH BRIDESMAID. *(To* 3RD BRIDESMAID*)* The Elks are in Bermuda.

3RD BRIDESMAID. *(To* 5TH BRIDESMAID*)* The Elks are in Bermuda.

5TH BRIDESMAID. *(Singing it)* The Elks are in Bermuda.

6TH BRIDESMAID. The farmer's in the dell. *(The offstage SAWING resumes.)*

BISHOP. There's a horse named Elk's Tooth running at Tia Juana. I think, just on a hunch, I'll——

MISS CHASEN. *(Entering up* L.*)* Is Doctor Lewis on the set?

(Together)

(KAMMERLING *enters* R.I, *followed by* 4TH BRIDESMAID *and* LEADING MAN *and* SCRIPT GIRL.)

KAMMERLING. Good morning! Good morning, everybody!

(Chorus of "Good mornning, Mr. Kammerling." 3RD *and* 6TH BRIDESMAIDS *rise.)*

(1ST CAMERAMAN *and* TRUCKMAN *clear chairs* C., *off* L.*)*

(2ND BRIDESMAID *enters up* C.*)*

KAMMERLING. Doctor Lewis here yet?

1ST CAMERAMAN. Nope.

6TH BRIDESMAID. Not yet.

5TH BRIDESMAID. No, he isn't, Miss Chasen.

MRS. WALKER. He's at the architect's.

MISS CHASEN. Well, Mr. Glogauer wants to know the minute he gets here. Will you have somebody let me know? *(Exits up* L.*)*

MRS. WALKER. He's at the architects. (KAM-MERLING *begins speaking through the rest of her line.*) I'll get Susan for you. *(Exits down* R.)

KAMMERLING. Now, listen, everybody. (JERRY *enters* R.I.) We take first the scene——

(The 4TH BRIDESMAID, *the* LEADING MAN, *and the* SCRIPT GIRL *have crossed to* L. *below the pews.* KAMMERLING *is down* C. *The* 2ND, 6TH, 5TH, 1ST, *and* 3RD BRIDESMAIDS *are lined up in that order from* R. *to* L. *between the altar and the pews. The* BISHOP *is standing below the second pew. The* 1ST LIGHT MAN *is on the platform behind the altar. The* 2ND LIGHT MAN *is at the altar. The* 2ND CAMERAMAN *is at the upstage camera* L. *The* 1ST CAMERAMAN *and* TRUCK-MAN *at the downstage camera. SAWING stops.)*

JERRY. Well, Kammerling——
KAMMERLING. Yes, Mr. Hyland——
JERRY. We're on the home stretch, eh?

KAMMERLING. That is right. (SUSAN *enters* R.I *in full bridal regalia, except for veil.*) We do first the retake on the steps.

SUSAN. *(Breaking in as she reaches* KAMMER-LING *and* JERRY) Oh, Mr. Kammerling, I'm ready to be shot!

KAMMERLING. Fine! We take the scene on the church steps.

SUSAN. The what?

KAMMERLING. The scene on the church steps.

SUSAN. But I don't think I know that scene.

JERRY. Didn't May rehearse you in that this morning?

SUSAN. No—she didn't.

KAMMERLING. Miss Daniels! Where is Miss Daniels?

VOICE. *(Off)* Miss Daniels on the set!

KAMMERLING. *(Crossing and exiting* R.I*)* She knew we were going to take it. *(Calling)* Miss Daniels——!

SUSAN. Jerry, did Mother tell you—we just had a telegram from Father?

JERRY. No. What's up?

6TH BRIDESMAID. He joined the Elks.

SUSAN. He's coming on for the wedding.

MAY. *(Entering* R.I) Does there seem to be some trouble here?

JERRY. May, what about the church steps? Susan says you didn't rehearse her. (KAMMERLING *enters* R.I.)

MAY. Hello, Jerry. Susan, I know your memory isn't very good, but I want you to think way back to—— Oh, pretty near five minutes ago. We were sitting in your dressing room—remember?—and we rehearsed that scene? (2ND CAMERAMAN *exits up* L.*)*

SUSAN. But that isn't the scene he means.

MAY. *(To* KAMMERLING*)* Outside the church, is that right?

KAMMERLING. Yes, yes!

SUSAN. Outside the church—— Oh, yes, we did *that!* You said the church steps.

KAMMERLING. That's right! That's right!

MAY. Susan—we feel that it's time you were told this. Outside the church and the church steps are really the same scene.

SUSAN. Are they?

MAY. Yes. In practically all churches now they put the steps on the outside.

SUSAN. Oh, I see. }
JERRY. Come on, May. } *(Together)*

KAMMERLING. Then are we ready?

MAY. Do you remember the scene as we just rehearsed it, Susan? You remember that you ascend four steps—then turn and wave to the crowd——

SUSAN. Oh, yes—now I remember! *(She waves her hand in a violent gesture.)*

MAY. No, no—you do not launch a battleship. You see, they'd have to get a lot of water for that— *(The offstage SAWING recommences.)*

KAMMERLING. Is it then settled what you are doing?

SUSAN. *(Starting to exit up L.)* Well, I think I understand. The steps are outside the church. *(Exits.)*

JERRY. May, I just came from Glogauer and what do you think?

MAY. What?

2ND BRIDESMAID. *(Coming down to JERRY)* Mr. Hyland, will we be working tonight?

JERRY. What?

2ND BRIDESMAID. *(Without waiting for JERRY's answer)* Lily, want to make a date tonight—those exhibitors are in town again.

KAMMERLING. All right! I want everybody on the church steps! Come on! *(The ACTORS start moving toward the exit up L.)* Everybody on Stage Thirty-one! Stage Thirty-one! Retake of the church steps! *(The CROWD is off, leaving only MAY and JERRY down C., the 2ND BRIDESMAID and the 5TH BRIDESMAID, who have lagged behind, and the 2ND LIGHT MAN, who is at the altar, gazing intently up into the flies. SAWING stops.)*

5TH BRIDESMAID. Who?

2ND BRIDESMAID. Those two exhibitors.

5TH BRIDESMAID. Oh, Mr. Hyland, do you want us tonight?

JERRY. Can't tell till later.

5TH BRIDESMAID. Well, I've got a chance to go out with an exhibitionist—— *(To 2ND BRIDESMAID)* I can't stay out late tonight—I've got to be home by dawn. *(By this time all are off except MAY and* JERRY. *Their scene is broken from time to time by the crossing of* STUDIO MEN *and* ACTORS. 2ND ELECTRICIAN *enters up* L.; *crosses; exits up* C.*)*

JERRY. Listen, May—Glogauer is tickled pink.

MAY. He must look lovely.

JERRY. Picture finished right on schedule, advancing the opening date—— It's the first time it ever happened!

MAY. Yah.

JERRY. You don't seem very excited about it. Picture opening in three days—and it's going to be a knockout, too.

MAY. *(Who has heard all this before)* Now, Jerry.

JERRY. Well, it is, and I don't care what you think.

MAY. But Jerry, use a little common sense. You've seen the rushes. What's the use of kidding yourself? (2ND LIGHT MAN *exits up* C.*)*

JERRY. All right. Everybody's wrong but you.

MAY. I can't help what I see, Jerry. The lighting, for example. Those big scenes where you can't see anything—everybody in shadow—what about those?

JERRY. That's only a few scenes. You know that —George forgot to tell them to turn the lights on, and they thought he meant it that way. Nobody'll notice it.

MAY. All right. But I caught something new yesterday. That knocking that goes on—did you get that?

JERRY. Well, we're trying to find out about that. The sound engineers are working on it.

MAY. Don't you know what that was?

JERRY. No. What?

MAY. That was George cracking his goddam Indian nuts. (2ND LIGHT MAN *enters up* C. *to platform. SAWING resumes.)*

JERRY. Is that what it was?

MAY. I suppose nobody's going to notice *that,* either.

(The THREE SCENARIO WRITERS *enter from* R.I, *talking as they come.)*

FULTON. But say, he's had it five weeks. He ought to know by this time.

MOULTON. Well, you can't push 'em—you know that. (SULLIVAN *interrupts with his line,* MOULTON *continuing)* Why, a couple of years ago——

SULLIVAN. Yeah—I left a scenario in an office once—— *(They are drowned out by the confusion of* GEORGE'S *entrance, but continue to talk regardless)* Say, this might be a darned good time to buttonhole him—

FULTON. Yeah, now we'll find out——

MOULTON. He's had it long enough——

VOICE. *(Off* L.) Doctor Lewis is coming!

VOICE. *(Nearer)* Doctor Lewis is coming! *(There is a good deal of noise and confusion as* GEORGE *enters from up* L., *followed by quite an entourage, bestowing cheery "Good mornings" to all and sundry. He is followed by his* SECRETARY, *laden with papers, and preceded by the* TWO PAGES, *bearing* GLO-GAUER'S *silver coffee service. Through his early lines in this scene he is drinking a cup of coffee and simultaneously carrying on important business with his* SECRETARY. *The* SECRETARY, *who is carrying a pile of slips, peels off one at a time and holds it in front of* GEORGE, *who indicates "Yes" or "No" with a shake of the head. Now and then a document is given to him to sign. A* PAGE *holds the coffee cup during this formality, then hands it back to him.)*

GEORGE. Good-morning! Good-morning, everybody! *(Responses from* ALL. *The* 2ND CAMERAMAN *has followed* GEORGE *on from* L.2. *The* 1ST CAMERAMAN *and the* TRUCKMAN *have entered* L.1. *The* 1ST *and* 5TH BRIDESMAIDS *have entered from up* C., *followed by the* BISHOP. *As soon as* GEORGE *is* C., KAMMERLING *enters from up* C., *followed by* SUSAN *and the* SCRIPT GIRL. MAY *and* JERRY *are* R.C., *near the altar. SAWING stops.)*

GEORGE. Hello, darling! Well, Kammerling! What have I done this morning?

KAMMERLING. We have taken the retake on the church steps.

GEORGE. Well, what else have I got to decide? *(Motions to* SECRETARY *for Indian nuts, which he receives.* GEORGE *takes coffee cup from* SECRETARY. PAGES *exit* L.2.)

KAMMERLING. There is only the last scene—the wedding ceremony.

JERRY. Right on schedule.

GEORGE. There's just the one scene left to take?

KAMMERLING. That is all.

GEORGE. *(A snap of the fingers; the decision has been reached)* We'll take that scene.

KAMMERLING. Everybody on the set, please! Everybody on the set! (STRAGGLERS *enter.)*

GEORGE. I'll decide everything else at two o'clock.

SECRETARY. *(Hands papers to* GEORGE *to sign)* Yes, sir.

MAY. *(Coming to* GEORGE*)* Doctor Lewis, I'm Miss Daniels. I met you in New York.

GEORGE. Hello, May.

MAY. How do you do?

KAMMERLING. Are we then ready? Ready, Doctor Lewis?

FULTON. Doctor Lewis, we left a scenario in your office——

SECRETARY. No answers on scenarios until two o'clock.

GEORGE. That's right.

MOULTON. But it's five weeks now.

FULTON. Oh, we might as well give up. (*The* THREE SCENARIO WRITERS *exit* R.I.)

KAMMERLING. All right, Doctor? Are we ready, Doctor?

GEORGE. All right. We'll take the scene from wherever it was left off.

(Together)

KAMMERLING. (*Announcing*) We will take the end of the wedding ceremony, where we left off! Places, please! We are going to take the end of the wedding ceremony. Everybody in their places. (*The* BISHOP, *the* LEADING MAN *and* SUSAN *take their places at the altar.*)

(The IST, 6TH *and* 2ND BRIDESMAIDS *range themselves below the altar, the* 5TH, 4TH *and* 3RD BRIDESMAIDS *above it,* ALL *looking directly at the cameras* L., *their backs to the* BISHOP *and the altar.* MRS. WALKER *enters up* L.2 *and crosses to* SUSAN *to arrange her veil.* JERRY *and* MAY *are down* L. *below the downstage camera.* GEORGE, *his* SECRETARY, *and the* SCRIPT GIRL *are* L.C., KAMMERLING *is* C. GEORGE *gives coffee cup to* SECRETARY, *who takes it off* L.I, *then re-enters.*)

KAMMERLING. (*To the* BISHOP) Oh, Mr. Jackson, have you got this straight?

GEORGE. *(Sternly)* Get this straight, Mr. Jackson.

BISHOP. *(At the altar)* What?

KAMMERLING. About the ceremony. You understand that when she says "I do," you release the pigeons. (1ST BRIDESMAID *sits on platform.*)

BISHOP. Oh, sure.

KAMMERLING. They are in that little cottage up there. When Miss Walker says "I do," you pull that ribbon and the pigeons will fly out.

BISHOP. They ain't gonna fly down on me again, are they?

KAMMERLING. No, no, they have been rehearsed.

GEORGE. Those pigeons know what to do. They were in "The Seven Commandments."

BISHOP. Oh, yeah—I was a rabbi in that one.

GEORGE. Oh! I forgot! There aren't any pigeons.

KAMMERLING. What?

GEORGE. Well, they had to stay up in there so long, and I felt kinda sorry for them, so I had them sent back to the man.

KAMMERLING. Well, what shall we do?

GEORGE. Well, as long as we haven't got any, we won't use them. That's what we'll do—we won't use pigeons.

KAMMERLING. Very well, Doctor.

MAY. He certainly meets emergencies.

SUSAN. Oh, George! Is that all I say?

GEORGE. What?

SUSAN. Is that all I say during the entire ceremony—just "I do"?

GEORGE. Is that all she says, May?

MAY. That's all. That's the part she knows, too.

SUSAN. But that's so short.

GEORGE. Yes!

MAY. Well, maybe she could perform the ceremony—then she could do all the talking.

GEORGE. But that wouldn't fit the scenario!

VOICE. *(Offstage* R.*)* Mr. Glogauer is coming! *(VOICE nearer)* Mr. Glogauer is coming! *(There is a general ad lib. on stage.)*

(GLOGAUER enters R.I, *followed by* TWO PAGES, ONE *carrying a small gold table on which there is a telephone with long cord attached, the* OTHER *carrying a stool. They are followed by* MISS CHASEN, *with her notebook. The* PAGES *set the table and chair below the altar and exit* R.I. *The* 1ST PAGE *carries the cord offstage to plug it in.* MISS CHASEN *immediately sits at the table. The* 5TH BRIDESMAID, *weary, sits in the first pew. The* BRIDESMAIDS *and* STAGE HANDS *relax.)*

GLOGAUER. Well! Here is the happy family! *(A general greeting.)* Well, everything going fine, huh?

JERRY. Right on schedule, Mr. Glogauer.

GEORGE. That's what it is.

GLOGAUER. Well, that's wonderful—wonderful. What's going on now?

GEORGE. We're taking the last scene.

GLOGAUER. That's fine—fine. I congratulate everybody.

MISS CHASEN. *(Into the telephone)* Miss Chasen speaking. Mr. Glogauer is on Number Nine.

GLOGAUER. Tell them I will look at "Foolish Virgins" at two-fifteen.

MISS CHASEN. Mr. Glogauer will look at "Foolish Virgins" at two-fifteen.

GLOGAUER. And the reason I came down is—— You don't mind if I interrupt you for a minute for a very special reason?

} *(Together)*

GEORGE. Why, no. *(There is a general movement.*

Some of the BRIDESMAIDS *sit on the steps of the altar.)*

GLOGAUER. Everybody stay here, please! I want everybody to hear this!

GEORGE. Everybody listen to Mr. Glogauer! Mr. Glogauer is probably going to say something.

KAMMERLING. Attention, everybody!

GLOGAUER. Boys and girls, as you know, this is the last day of the shooting. Many of you have worked for me before, but never under such happy circumstances, and so I want you all to be here while I say something. Seventeen years ago—— *(The* BISHOP, *with a sigh, sits in the large chair at the altar.)* —when I went into the movie business, I made up my mind it should be run like a business, as a business, and for a business. And that is what I have tried to do. But never before have I been able to do it until today. Never since I started to make Glogauer Super-Jewels has a picture of mine been finished exactly on the schedule. And what is the reason for that? Because now for the first time we have a man who is able to make decisions, and to make them like that—— *(A snap of the fingers)* —Doctor George Lewis. (ALL *applaud.)*

GEORGE. *(As the applause dies)* Ladies and Gentlemen——

GLOGAUER. Wait a minute—I am not through yet. (GEORGE *apologetically steps back.)* And so in recognition of his remarkable achievement, I take great pleasure in presenting him with a very small token of my regard. *(He signals to someone offstage* L.2. *Immediately* TWO ELECTRICIANS *enter, carrying a huge table on which is spread out a golden dinner set, something absolutely staggering. It is met with a chorus of delighted little gasps.* SUSAN *scampers down to gurgle over it.)* A solid gold dinner set, a hundred and six pieces, and with his initials in diamonds on every piece. *(There is a general AP-*

PLAUSE, and the 1ST, 3RD, 4TH *and* 5TH BRIDES-
MAIDS *run over to inspect it at close range.)*

MAY. What's the *first* prize? *(There are calls of
"Speech" and "Doctor Lewis.")*

GEORGE. Ladies and Gentlemen—and Mr. Glogauer—this is the first solid gold dinner set I have
ever received. I hardly know what to say, because
this is the first solid gold dinner set I have ever received, and I hardly know what to say. All I can say
is it's wonderful, Mr. Glogauer, and now let's show
Mr. Glogauer the finish of the picture, and take the
last scene. *(The* 2ND ELECTRICIAN *takes position at
lamp on platform down* R.*)*

KAMMERLING. *(Pushing the* BRIDESMAIDS *away
from the dinner set)* All right, all right! Look at it
afterwards! (MISS CHASEN *rises. The* TWO PAGES
*enter and remove the table, telephone and stool, and
exit.* TRUCKMAN *and* 1ST CAMERAMAN *move dinner
set upstage.)*

GLOGAUER. *(As* MISS CHASEN *starts to exit)* I
will address the new playwrights on Number Eight.

MISS CHASEN. Yes, Mr. Glogauer.

KAMMERLING. Everybody take their places! Mr.
Glogauer is waiting.

GEORGE. Everybody take their places! (BISHOP,
LEADING MAN, SUSAN *and* BRIDESMAIDS *take places
at the altar.)*

1ST LIGHT MAN. Hey, Spike!

BISHOP. Yah?

1ST LIGHT MAN. They're off at Caliente. Fourth
race.

BISHOP. O. K. Let me know the minute you
hear.

1ST LIGHT MAN. O. K.

KAMMERLING. All right. We are taking the scene
now, Mr. Jackson. Horses come later.

GEORGE. We are taking the scene now, Mr. Glogauer.

GLOGAUER. Fine!

KAMMERLING. Are we lined? (CAMERAMEN *assent.*) Phrased? *(Another assent.)* Red light. How are we for sound?

MIXER. *(Through phone)* O. K.

KAMMERLING. All right. Are we up to speed?

VOICE. *(Off)* Right.

KAMMERLING. Four bells! *(FOUR BELLS sound. Complete silence.)*

VOICE. *(Offstage)* Taking on upper stage!

VOICE. *(Further off)* Taking on upper stage! Everybody quiet!

KAMMERLING. Hit your lights! *(LIGHTS on.)* Camera!

BISHOP. Cyril Fonsdale, dost thou take this woman to be thy wedded wife, to live together in the holy state of matrimony? Dost thou promise within sacred sight of this altar to love her, comfort her, honor and keep her in sickness and in health, and, forsaking all others, keep true only unto her, so long as ye both shall live?

LEADING MAN. I do.

BISHOP. Mildred Martin, dost thou take this man to be thy wedded husband? Dost thou promise to obey him and serve him, love, honor and keep him, in sickness and in health, so long as ye both shall live?

SUSAN. I do.

BISHOP. Forasmuch as these two have consented together in holy wedlock, and have witnessed the same before this company and have given and pedged their troth each to the other, I hereby pronounce them man and wife. (SUSAN *and* LEADING MAN *embrace as camera on truck is moved up for close-up.)*

KAMMERLINC Cut! One bell! *(ONE BELL sounds.)*

1ST LIGHT MAN. Spike!

BISHOP. Yeah?

1ST LIGHT MAN. That horse ran sixth.

BISHOP. God damn it! I knew that would happen. *(HAMMERING and SAWING resume.)*

GEORGE. There you are, Mr. Glogauer—— *(HAMMERING and SAWING stop.)* Embrace, fade-out, the end.   *(LIGHTS out.)*

GLOGAUER. I see, I see. Wait a minute—I don't understand. You said what?

GEORGE. Embrace, fade-out, the end.

GLOGAUER. End? You mean you take this scene last. But it's not really the end.

GEORGE. Sure it is. *(To KAMMERLING and OTHERS)* Isn't it?

KAMMERLING. Certainly it's the end.

GLOGAUER. But how can it be? What about the backstage scene?

KAMMERLING. What?

GLOGAUER. *(Slightly frenzied)* On the opening night! When her mother is dying, and she has to act anyhow!

GEORGE. That wasn't in it, Mr. Glogauer.

KAMMERLING. Why, no.

GLOGAUER. Wasn't in it! I had twelve playwrights working on that.

GEORGE. But it wasn't in it.

GLOGAUER. *(Dangerously calm)* This is a picture about a little country girl!

GEORGE. Yes, sir.

GLOGAUER. Who gets a job in a Broadway cabaret?

GEORGE. There isn't any Broadway cabaret.

GLOGAUER. No Broadway cabaret?

GEORGE. She doesn't come to New York in this.

GLOGAUER. Doesn't come—— You mean the cabaret owner doesn't make her go out with this bootlegger?

GEORGE. Why, no, Mr. Glogauer.

GLOGAUER. Well, what happens to her? What *does* she do?

GEORGE. Why, this rich woman stops off at the farmhouse and she takes her to Florida and dresses her all up.

GLOGAUER. And there is no backstage scene? Any place?

GEORGE. No. She goes in swimming and gets too far out and then Cyril Fonsdale happens to come—

GLOGAUER. Let me see that script, please. (SCRIPT GIRL *hands* GLOGAUER *the script.*)

GEORGE. It's all there, Mr. Glogauer. (GLOGAUER *looks through script.*) See?—There's where she goes swimming. *(Points to page; cracks nut.)*

GLOGAUER. *(Pages through the script. A moment's pause, then he slams it shut)* Do you know what you have done, Doctor Lewis? You have made the wrong picture!

GEORGE. Huh?
KAMMERLING. What is that? } *(Together)*

GLOGAUER. That is all you have done! Made the wrong picture!

GEORGE. But—but——
JERRY. Are you sure, Mr. Glogauer? } *(Together)*

GLOGAUER. *(Looking at the thing in his hand)* Where did you get such a script?

GEORGE. Why, it's the one you gave me.

GLOGAUER. I never gave you such a script. She goes swimming! Swimming! Do you know who made this picture? Biograph, in 1910! Florence Lawrence, and Maurice Costello—and even then it was no good!

GEORGE. Well, everybody was here while we were making it.

GLOGAUER. Everybody was here! Where were their minds? Kammerling! Kammerling!

KAMMERLING. It is not my fault. Doctor Lewis gave us the script.

GLOGAUER. I had to bring you all the way from Germany for this! Miss Newton! You held the script in your hands. Where were your eyes?

SCRIPT GIRL. I got it from Doctor Lewis—right in his office. I'm sure I couldn't——

GLOGAUER. So, Doctor! On Wednesday night we open and we have *got* to open! And after that it goes to four hundred exhibitors and we got signed contracts! So tell me what to do, please!

GEORGE. Well—well, what do you think we ought to do?

GLOGAUER. Never in my life have I known such a thing. After this I make a ruling—every scenario we produce, somebody has got to read it.

JERRY. Yes, Mr. Glogauer.

GLOGAUER. You know what this does to *you*, Miss Walker! You are through! Swimming! This kills your career! And you know who you got to thank for it? Doctor Lewis! (GEORGE *crosses to* SUSAN. SUSAN *meets the situation by bursting into tears.*) A fine supervisor! The business is in the hands of incompetents, he says! So what do I do? I give him everything the way he wants it—his own star—his own staff—— (*It is a new thought. He fixes* MAY *and* JERRY *with his eyes, crosses to them*) Oh, yes. And where were you people while all this was going on?

JERRY. (*Hastily*) Mr. Glogauer, I was on the cost end. I didn't have anything to do with the script. Doctor Lewis was the——

GLOGAUER. But Miss Daniels was here—all the time! Right with Doctor Lewis! (*To* MAY) What about *that?*

MAY. (*Not frightened*) Yes. I was here.

GLOGAUER. Well! Where was your mind?

MAY. To tell you the truth, Mr. Glogauer, I thought it was just another Super-Jewel.

GLOGAUER. Oh, you did?

MAY. I couldn't see any difference.

GLOGAUER. You couldn't, huh?

MAY. And while we're on the subject, Mr. Glogauer, just why is it all Doctor Lewis's fault?

GLOGAUER. Why is it his fault? Who did this thing? Who else is to blame?

MAY. Well, if I'm not too inquisitive, what do *you* do with yourself all the time? Play marbles?

GLOGAUER. What's that?

MAY. Where were *you* while all this was going on? Out to lunch?

GLOGAUER. *(Drawing himself up with dignity)* I go to my office. That will be all. *(About to say something else, but changes his mind)* I go to my office. *(Notices the script still in his hand; crosses to* GEORGE*)* Mr. Supervisor, I make you a present. *(Hands script to* GEORGE.*)*

GEORGE. *(Weakly, as he takes it)* Thank you.

GLOGAUER. *(To the* COMPANY*)* And will you all please understand that nothing about this is to get out of the studio. That is official. *(Starts to exit* R.I*)* Come, Hyland! Seventeen years and this is the worst thing that has ever happened to me!

JERRY. *(Following him off)* Mr. Glogauer, if I'd been on the set this never would have happened. But I didn't have anything to do with the script— I never even saw—— *(He is off.)*

KAMMERLING. *(After a moment's pause)* That is all for today. You will be notified.

BISHOP. *(Starting to go)* Well—the wrong picture and the wrong horse! *(A BABBLE of talk springs up as* EVERYONE *starts to go.* SUSAN *has a fresh outburst of tears.)*

GEORGE. Susan, don't cry like that.

SUSAN. *(Through sobs)* You heard what Mr. Glogauer said—my career is ruined. I'm—through. *(She exits* R.I.*)*

MRS. WALKER. *(Following her, and breaking in*

her speech) Now, darling, you mustn't take on that way. Everything'll turn out all right. *(Exits R·I.)*

GEORGE. *(Through the* OTHERS' *speeches)* But, Susan, it wasn't my fault. I didn't know it was the wrong picture. *(Exits R.I. The* OTHERS *are also exiting, talking as they go. The NOISE gradually subsides. All are now off except* MAY *and* KAMMERLING.*)*

KAMMERLING. It is too bad, Miss Daniels.

MAY. Yah. Isn't it.

KAMMERLING. But after all it is the movie business. It is just the same in Germany.

MAY. It is, huh?

KAMMERLING. Even worse. Oh, it is terrible over there. I think I go back. (GEORGE'S SECRETARY *enters* R.I, *whistling; crosses. He exits up* C.*)*

JERRY. *(Starting in at white heat—enters at end of musical phrase from* R.I) Well, you fixed everything fine, didn't you? On top of everything else you had to go and get smart!

MAY. It was time somebody got smart, Jerry.

JERRY. Well you *did* it! And maybe you think Glogauer isn't sore.

MAY. Well, you don't have to worry, do you, Jerry?

JERRY. What?

MAY. *(Very calmly)* You don't have to worry. You crawled out from under. You gave as pretty an exhibition as *I've* ever seen.

JERRY. What do you mean?

MAY. Oh, nothing. Just the way you stood up for George.

JERRY. Well, somebody's got to keep his feet on the ground around here!

MAY. *(So quietly)* Yours are all right—aren't they, Jerry? Yah. Right deep in the soil of California!

JERRY. I was trying to fix things up—that's what I was trying to do.

MAY. No, Jerry. No. It's been coming on you ever since you got out here, and now it's here. You've gone Hollywood, Jerry. And as far as I'm concerned, that's that. *(It has been said very quietly, but its very quietness gives it a definiteness.* JERRY *looks at her; senses that she means it. He turns on his heel and goes out* L.I. MAY *is alone for a moment. Then offstage, up* L., *a* MAN'S *VOICE is heard, singing, "I wanna be loved by you-ou-ou, and nobody else but you. I wanna be kissed by you, a-lone." On the word "alone" the* SINGER *comes into sight* C. *It is the* BISHOP, *holding up his robes to keep from tripping, and disappears up* C.)

GEORGE. *(Enters* R.I) She wouldn't talk to me, May! Shut the door right in my face and wouldn't talk to me!

MAY. *(Abstracted)* What?

GEORGE. She just keeps on crying and won't even talk to me.

MAY. That's all right. Everything is all right. It is for me, anyhow. Just fine and dandy.

GEORGE. Fine and dandy?   *(WARN Curtain.)*

MAY. Just swell.

GEORGE. Susan ought to know I didn't do it on purpose. I tried to tell her. Look, May, do you think the picture's so bad?

MAY. Bad as what, George?

GEORGE. Bad as he thinks it is?

MAY. Well, I think it's got a good chance.

GEORGE. Chance of what, May?

MAY. Of being as bad as he thinks it is.

GEORGE. Oh!

MAY. By the way, George—just to keep the record straight—how'd you come to *make* the wrong picture? Or don't you know?

GEORGE. Well, I've been trying to think. You know that thing in my office where we keep the new scenarios? Well, if you're in a hurry it looks just like the wastebasket, and so I reached into it—only it was the wastebasket.

MAY. Well, you certainly produced it.

MISS CHASEN. *(Heard offstage)* Paging Doctor Lewis! Miss Daniels!

MAY. Ah, here we are! Right in here. I thought it was taking a long time. (MISS CHASEN *enters* R.I.) You're late.

MISS CHASEN. *(Giving her two envelopes)* Executive office! No answer! *(Turns to go.)*

MAY. Wait a minute. Who else have you got? *(Examining remaining envelopes)* Kammerling, Weisskopf, Meterstein—— Ah, yes. (MISS CHASEN *exits* R.I. MAY *turns back to* GEORGE) Do you want yours?

GEORGE. Do you mean we're—fired, May?

MAY. Good and fired!

GEORGE. *(In a daze, opening his letter)* Yah.

MAY. *(Looking at hers) Me too.* Well, George— *(Crossing a step* L., *then turning to* GEORGE) —we've got a solid gold dinner set, anyway. (Two PAGES *enter up* L. *and carry off the dinner set.)* A hundred and six pieces, and every piece marked with your initials in diamonds. That's not bad for two months—— (MAY *turns in time to see the dinner set disappear)* Well, anyway, George—— *(The CURTAIN starts to fall.)* You *did* have a solid gold dinner set, a hundred and six pieces——

THE CURTAIN IS DOWN

ACT THREE

SCENE II: *The Pullman car again.*

> *At the rise the scene is empty. After a moment the* PORTER *enters* L., *pushes a bag under the seat* L.C. *and starts to cross to* R. *As he reaches* R.C. *the train WHISTLES for a crossing. Outside the window, a light effect, as of a moving train.*

(MAY enters L., *picks up book, sits seat* L. *in* L. *section.)*

PORTER. You ready to have your berth made up?

MAY. No, thanks.

PORTER. *(Crosses* L. *to* C.*)* I been meaning to ask you, Miss Daniels—how's come those two gentlemen ain't going back?

MAY. Well, that's a long story.

PORTER. Yes, ma'am.

MAY. But I wouldn't be surprised if at least one of them was with you pretty soon. *(The train WHISTLE blows for a stop. The EFFECT begins to slow. The train WHISTLE blows.)*

PORTER. We makes a two-minute stop here. Anything you want?

MAY. No, thanks. Where are we?

PORTER. We makes a stop at Needle's Point. That's where they got that sanitarium.

MAY. Look—is there a news stand?

PORTER. Yes, ma'am.

MAY. See if you can get hold of Thursday's Los Angeles papers, will you?

PORTER. Yes, ma'am. *(Starts off L.)*

MAY. *(Calls after him)* They've got to be Thursday's or I don't want 'em. (MAY *is left alone. There is a single blast of the WHISTLE. The LIGHTS no longer fly past outside the window. Again* MAY *tries to look out. Then she settles herself again; takes up the book; tries to read; throws it down. The* PORTER *re-enters L. with luggage.)*

PORTER. Right this way, sir. You need any help? *(To* MAY*)* Just a gentleman from the sanitarium. Right this way, sir.

(LAWRENCE VAIL *enters L. Instantly, of course, he recognizes* MAY.)

MAY. *(Rises. The* PORTER *exits L.)* Why, Mr. Vail!

VAIL. Hello, Miss Daniels.

MAY. So you're the gentleman from the sanitarium?

VAIL. That's right. Well, this is certainly a surprise.

MAY. Well—please sit down.

VAIL. Thanks.—Well!

MAY. *(Sitting)* You're certainly the last person— I hadn't heard you were ill. Nothing serious, I hope?

VAIL. *(Shakes his head)* Just a kind of breakdown. *(Sits)* Underwork.

MAY. I can't quite picture that reception room without you.

VAIL. Then I heard about this place—sanitarium here. Sounded pretty good, so I came out. Fellow named Jenkins runs it. Playwright. Seems he came out here to write scenarios, but he couldn't stand the sitting. Went mad in the eighth month. So he started this place. Doesn't take anything but playwrights.

MAY. Good, is it?

VAIL. Great. First three days they put you in a room without a chair in it. Then they have a big art gallery—life-size portraits of all the studio executives. You see, for an hour every day you go in there and say whatever you want to any picture.

MAY. *(Nods)* I see.

PORTER. *(Enters L.)* I'll get your papers right now. *(Exit R.)*

VAIL. And now what's all this about? Going home on a visit?

MAY. Well—going home.

VAIL. All washed up?

MAY. Scrubbed.

VAIL. Really? I'm kind of surprised. I never quite got the hang of what you people did out there, but I had the idea you were in pretty solid. Something happen?

MAY. *(Taking a moment)* Did you ever meet Doctor Lewis?

VAIL. Yes. I had quite a talk with Doctor Lewis.

MAY. Well, Doctor Lewis did something that no one had ever done before. He reminded Mr. Glogauer about turning the Vitaphone down. That made him supervisor.

VAIL. Only supervisor?

MAY. And there was also Miss Susan Walker. Miss Walker is a young woman who has a chance of becoming the world's worst actress. I should say a very good chance. She's young yet—and getting worse right along.

VAIL. I see.

MAY. With that to start with, the Doctor cinched things by working from the wrong scenario. Some little thing from 1910. The picture opened Wednesday. And how is *your* uncle, Mr. Vail?

VAIL. My recollection of the 1910 pictures is that they weren't so bad.

MAY. They didn't have the Doctor in those days. Most of it you can't see because the Doctor forgot to tell them to turn the lights on. Miss Walker has a set of gestures that would do credit to a travelling derrick—and did you ever happen to hear about the Doctor's bright particular weakness?

VAIL. Is there something else?

MAY. It's called Indian nuts. *(A glance at the seats)* There must be one around here somewhere. Anyhow, he eats them. With sound. He kept cracking them right through the picture, and they recorded swell.

VAIL. That, I take it, decided you?

MAY. That, and—other things.

VAIL. Funny—I should think there would be a great field out there for a man who could turn out the wrong picture.

MAY. *(Leaning back)* Yes—if he could do it regularly. But sooner or later Doctor Lewis would make the right one and spoil everything.

VAIL. Not the Doctor.

MAY. Well, maybe you're right.

PORTER. *(Re-entering R. with two newspapers and a pillow)* Here your papers, Miss Daniels.

MAY. *(Taking them)* Thanks.

PORTER. *(To VAIL)* I brought you a pillow.

VAIL. *(Putting it on seat beside him)* Thank you. (PORTER *exits* R. *A look after him.)*

MAY. *(Scanning the date line)* Yah. These have probably got the notices. *(Extending them toward VAIL.)*

VAIL. *(Reaching for one)* Oh, you mean the picture?

MAY. It wouldn't surprise me. *(They each open
a paper.* MAY *is in no hurry.)*

VAIL. You're a pretty brave girl, actually sending
out for these.

MAY. Well, I might as well know the worst.

VAIL. *(Finding the place)* Here we are, I guess.
"Gingham and Orchids"—that the name of it?

MAY. That's it.

VAIL. *(Scanning the headlines as he folds the
paper)* An all-talking, all-singing——

MAY. All-lousy picture. (MAY *takes the paper,*
VAIL *meanwhile opening the other one.)*

VAIL. *(As* MAY *reads)* Yes, I guess that must be
what they mean by a hundred percent. (MAY's *eyes
slide quickly down the column, then she looks blank-
ly up at* VAIL, *who is opening the other paper)*
What is it? (MAY *hands the paper over to him, indicating the spot.* VAIL *reads)* "Never in the history of Hollywood has so tumultuous an ovation
been accorded to any picture——"

MAY. *(Not quite able to speak, indicates a spot
further on in the review)* Down there.

VAIL. *(Reads)* "Herman Glogauer's 'Gingham
and Orchids' is a welcome relief from the avalanche
of backstage pictures. It marks a turning point in
the motion picture industry—*(A look at* MAY*)*—a
return to the sweet simplicity and tender wistful-
ness of yesteryear."

MAY. It *does* say that?

VAIL. *(Extending the paper to her)* Don't take
my word for it.

MAY. "A new star twinkled across the cinema
heavens last night and the audience took her to its
heart. Here at last is an actress who is not afraid
to appear awkward and ungraceful." *(Pointing)*
That word is "afraid," isn't it?

VAIL. That's what it is,

MAY. "In the scene on the church steps, where she waved to the onlookers below, her hands revealed a positively Duse-like quality." I'll tell you about that some day. *(Takes paper from* VAIL.*)*

VAIL. I'll be there.

MAY. *(Still reading)* "And here is one wedding, by the way, that sets a new mark for originality and freshness. It does not use pigeons." *(An unbelieving shake of the head. Continues)* "Then, too, the lighting of the picture is superb. Doctor Lewis has wisely seen the value of leaving the climax to the imagination of the audience. In the big scenes almost nothing was visible." *(A pause. She indicates the other paper)* I'm afraid I haven't got strength enough to reach for that one. (VAIL *hands the other paper to* MAY.*)*

VAIL. I beg your pardon—— *(Reaching for first paper, which is on seat beside* MAY*)* I don't suppose the whole thing—*(Indicating the review)*—could be a typographical error, could it?

MAY. *(Looks it quickly over, then looks up at* VAIL *with a weak smile)* I want you to settle yourself for this.   *(WARN Curtain.)*

VAIL. I'm ready.

MAY. Put the pillow right back of you.

VAIL. All right. *(Does so.)*

MAY. "In the opening sequences the audience was puzzled by a constant knocking, and it seemed to many of us that something might be wrong with the sound apparatus. Then suddenly we realized that what was being done was what Eugene O'Neill did with the constant beating of the tom-tom in 'The Emperor Jones.' It was the beat of the hail on the roof." *(She looks up at* VAIL, *who nods.* MAY *resumes reading)* "It is another of the masterly touches brought to the picture by that new genius of the films, Doctor George Lewis." *(She lowers the paper, then, as if she cannot quite believe it, raises it and reads again. For a moment* MAY *and* VAIL *merely look at each other. Then* VAIL *leans back, crosses his legs, sighs.)*

VAIL. I hear the boll weevil is getting into the cotton crop again.

PORTER. *(Returns R.)* Here's a telegram for you, Miss Daniels. Caught us right here at Needle's Point.

MAY. Oh, thanks. (PORTER *goes out* L.) My guess is that this is from that new genius of the films.

VAIL. I wouldn't wonder.

MAY. *(A glance at the telegram)* Yes. *(Reads)* "The picture is colossal—it has put the movies back where they were ten years ago—I am the Wonder Man of the Talkies. They keep coming at me to decide things. Please take next train back. Jerry is gone and I am all alone here. They have made me an Elk and Susan is an Eastern Star. Please take next train back. I need you. Where is Jerry? I am also a Shriner."

VAIL. Well, what are you going to do about that?

MAY. *(Looking at the telegram)* "Jerry is gone and I am all alone here." *(Letting the telegram slowly fall)* Well, it looks as if I'm going back.

VAIL. I think you have to.

MAY. Because if George is all alone out there— *(She breaks off)* And then there's another thing. As long as George owns Hollywood now, there are two or three reforms that I'd like to put into effect. Do you know what I'm going to do?

VAIL. What?

MAY. *(With gradually increasing momentum)* I'm going to get all those page boys together and take their signs away from them—then nobody will know where anybody is. I'm going to pack up the Schlepkins and send 'em back to Brooklyn, and then I'm going to bring their mother out *here*. I'm going to take Miss Leighton out of that reception room—

VAIL. Put cushions on those chairs——

MAY. And make her ask for an appointment to get back in.

VAIL. Great!

MAY. And when I get that done I'm going out to Mr. Glogauer's house, put the illuminated dome where the bathroom is—— *(The Curtain starts down.)*

MAY. *(Continuing)* And then I'm going to take the bathroom and drop it into the Pacific Ocean, and after that I'm going to make four trips and bring something back with me each time——

VAIL. *(Chiming in, talking simultaneously)* And then you can take the bathroom and put it where Glogauer is and then take Glogauer and do as your fancy bids you.

(Together)

THE CURTAIN IS DOWN

ACT THREE

SCENE III

The Reception Room again. Pictures of GEORGE
*over each door, which illuminate when the
doors are opened and closed.*

GEORGE, *very dressy, pacing up and down.*
SCRIPT GIRL *there with scripts.* GEORGE'S
SECRETARY *with a watch out. A* REPORTER *with
paper and pencil. A* MAN *sketching* GEORGE'S
portrait. A MAN *wanting an indorsement for
neckties.* 1ST PAGE *with Indian nuts. Everything going on at once, almost* EVERYONE *talking at once.*

GEORGE. So far as my plans for Mr. Glogauer
are concerned, I can only say that the coming year
will be a Glogauer year. (METERSTEIN *enters* R.2.)
And by the time all of our plans have been carried
into effect, why, the legitimate stage had better look
to its laurels. (MISS CHASEN *enters* R.I ; *exits* L.2.)

METERSTEIN. They're waiting for you on Number Eight, Doctor Lewis. (2ND PAGE *enters* L.2 *with
sign,* "MR. GLOGAUER IS ON NUMBER
FOUR.")

SECRETARY. Doctor Lewis on Number Eight **at**
three-twenty!

METERSTEIN. Right! *(Exits* R.2.)

PAINTER. *(Rises)* Doctor Lewis, **will you turn
your head just a little this way?**

BIOGRAPHER. *(Rises)* Doctor Lewis, we were up to Chapter Seven. September, 1910.

GEORGE. Oh, yes. My biography. I was still living in Medallion then. I was but a boy, and one day an idea came to me. I decided to be an usher.

TIE MAN. Doctor Lewis, your indorsement will have a hundred thousand men wearing Non-Wrinkable Ties inside of three months.

1ST REPORTER. Doctor Lewis, can I have the rest of that statement?

SECRETARY. *(Watch in hand)* One minute more, Doctor!

SCRIPT GIRL. Doctor Lewis, I have to have a decision on these scenarios. *(Down R.)*

PAINTER. Doctor Lewis, please! ⎱ *(Together)*
REPORTER. Doctor, it's getting late. ⎰

WEISSKOPF. *(Entering R.2)* O. K. on those contracts, Doctor!

GEORGE. O.K.! (WEISSKOPF *exits* L.2.)

1ST REPORTER. How about a statement from Miss Walker?

GEORGE. Well, Miss Walker is making a personal appearance in San Francisco. She'll be here pretty soon.

SECRETARY. Time! Time's up. (SCRIPT GIRL *exits* R.I.)

MISS LEIGHTON. *(Enters L.I)* Doctor Lewis, the Knights of Columbus are downstairs.

SECRETARY. Your time is up, gentlemen! Sorry!

REPORTER. Well, can we see him again later? ⎫
PAINTER. I'm only half finished here. ⎬ *(Together)*
TIE MAN. If I could have just one minute—— ⎭

SECRETARY. *(Shepherding them out)* The Doctor has no free time this month. All requests must be submitted in writing. *(Exit* REPORTERS, TIE MAN, PAINTER, L.I.)

MISS LEIGHTON. What about the Knights of Columbus, Doctor Lewis? Shall I tell them to come up?

GEORGE. Tell them I'll join later.

MISS LEIGHTON. Yes, sir. *(Goes out* L.I.)

GEORGE. Now, where were we?

BIOGRAPHER. You decided to be an usher.

GEORGE. I became an usher and pretty soon I was put in charge of the last two rows of the mezzanine.

SUSAN. *(Enters* L.I) Hello, George.

GEORGE. Hello, darling! *(Dismissing the* OTHERS*)* All right, everybody!

SECRETARY. All right. You are due on Number Eight in two minutes, Doctor.

GEORGE. All right.

SECRETARY. The Doctor will start Chapter Eight on Tuesday at twelve-fifteen. *(Exit* SECRETARY, BIOGRAPHER *and* PAGE L.2.)

GEORGE. How was it, Susan?

SUSAN. Oh, wonderful, George! Thousands of people, and arc lights, and my name on top of everything! Oh, it was wonderful, George!

GEORGE. It's been wonderful here, too. I'm up to Chapter Eight in my biography, and there's a man painting my portrait, and—— Oh, what do you think? I've got a surprise for you, Susan.

SUSAN. George, what is it? Tell me quick!

GEORGE. Three guesses.

SUSAN. A swimming pool?

GEORGE. No.

SUSAN. Two swimming pools?

GEORGE. It's an aeroplane.

SUSAN. George!

GEORGE. The man gave it to me for nothing. All I had to do was buy a few aeroplanes for Mr. Glogauer.

SUSAN. That's wonderful, George! Just what we needed!

GEORGE. First I was only going to buy a couple, but the man kept talking to me, and it worked out that if I bought a few more I'd get one free.

SUSAN. George, you're so clever. You couldn't have given me a nicer surprise. Isn't everything wonderful, George?

GEORGE. Yes, it is, only I wish May and Jerry would get here. They always know what to do in case things come up.

SUSAN. George, you mustn't worry about it. They got your telegrams.

GEORGE. Yes, but you see, Susan, we've always been together. This is the first time in years I haven't been together, and—— Did you see my pictures, Susan? They light up! *(Points to door* L.2 *as* GLOGAUER *enters with* MISS CHASEN*)* See?

GLOGAUER. Doctor Lewis, I want to talk to you. How do you do, Miss Walker? Doctor Lewis, did you order four hundred and sixty aeroplanes?

GEORGE. How's that?

GLOGAUER. Four hundred and sixty aeroplanes have just arrived in front of the studio. They say you ordered them.

GEORGE. Well, don't you believe in aviation, Mr. Glogauer?

GLOGAUER. The question is, Doctor Lewis, why did you buy four hundred and sixty aeroplanes?

MISS LEIGHTON. *(Enters* L.I*)* Mr. Glogauer! Another hundred aeroplanes just arrived and there's more coming every minute.

GLOGAUER. *What?*

MISS LEIGHTON. They're arriving in groups of fifty, Mr. Glogauer.

GLOGAUER. What is this, Doctor? Don't tell me you bought *more* than four hundred and sixty aeroplanes.

MISS LEIGHTON. The man from the aeroplane company says the order calls for two thousand!

GLOGAUER. Two thousand! Two thousand!

MISS LEIGHTON. That's what he said!

GLOGAUER. Is this *true,* Doctor? Can such a thing be possible?

GEORGE. Well, the man from the aeroplane company——

GLOGAUER. Two thousand! Two thousand aeroplanes! I want everybody in my office immediately! *(Starting for door* L.2*)* Meterstein—Weisskopf!

MISS CHASEN. *(Going out* L.2*)* Mr. Weisskopf! Mr. Meterstein!

GLOGAUER. *(Continuing as he exits)* Two thousand aeroplanes! Seventeen years and never in my life—— *(Storming out* L.2.*)*

MISS LEIGHTON. *(Following him out* L.2*)* I told them you weren't in and that you couldn't see anybody.

SUSAN. *(Also following off* L.2*)* George, is anything the matter? Shouldn't you have bought the aeroplanes?

GEORGE. *(Bringing up the rear)* But Mr. Glogauer, I don't see what you're so angry about! All I did was buy a few aeroplanes!

(ALL *are off. A pause. Then* MAY *enters* L.1. *She at once becomes conscious of the pictures of* GEORGE. *Looks at the lighted picture over the door through which she has entered. Closes the door, then opens and closes it again, to see it light. Crosses to up* R.C. *as* MISS LEIGHTON *returns* L.2.*)*

MISS LEIGHTON. Hello, Miss Daniels.

MAY. Hello, Miss Leighton.

MISS LEIGHTON. Have you been away?

MAY. *(Indicating the pictures)* I see you've got

some new decorations. *(She opens and closes the door* R.2.*)*

MISS LEIGHTON. How's that?

MAY. *(Trying the door. Referring to pictures of* GEORGE*)* Is that all they do? No fireworks?

MISS LEIGHTON. Aren't they lovely? Mr. Glogauer had them put up all over the building the day after the picture opened. When Doctor Lewis came into the studio, everything lit up.

MAY. Mr. Glogauer, too?

MISS LEIGHTON. How's that?

MAY. Miss Leighton—is—Mr. Hyland around?

MISS LEIGHTON. Mr. Hyland? Oh, Mr. Hyland isn't with us any more.

MAY. He isn't? Where is he?

MISS LEIGHTON. I don't know, Miss Daniels. I only know he isn't with the company. I think he went back East.

MAY. Went back East? When did he leave, Miss Leighton?

MISS LEIGHTON. Well, I really don't know, Miss Daniels——

MISS CHASEN. *(Entering* R.2*)* Miss Leighton, Mr. Glogauer wants his coffee. He's going crazy.

MISS LEIGHTON. But he's had it twice this morning.

MISS CHASEN. He wants it over again—he's absolutely raving. *(Exits* R.2.*)*

MISS LEIGHTON. Oh, dear! That's the second time this week he's raved. *(Exits* R.2.*)*

GEORGE. *(Enters* L.2*)* May!

MAY. Well, if it isn't Doctor Lewis!

GEORGE. Gosh, but I'm glad to see you, May! Did you—did you get my telegrams? I've been wiring you and wiring you.

MAY. Where's Jerry, George?

GEORGE. Why—why, I don't know. Isn't **he** with **you,** May? He went to find *you.*

MAY. Went where? When?

GEORGE. Why—why, right after you did. He had a big fight with Mr. Glogauer—he told him all kinds of things—and then he went looking for you, but you were gone already.

MAY. Wait a minute, George. You mean Jerry got fired?

GEORGE. *(Nods)* He didn't even get a letter.

MAY. Well, where is he now, George? Where did he go? Haven't you heard from him?

GEORGE. I don't know. Look, May, something terrible has happened. I bought a lot of aeroplanes—

MAY. George, where would Jerry be likely to go to? What did he say when he left here?

GEORGE. He didn't say anything, May. He just said he was going to find you and nothing else mattered.

MAY. Oh, he didn't say anything, eh? Just that?

GEORGE. He'll come back, May—he'll come back when he knows you're here. But May, what am I going to do about the aeroplanes? *(He breaks off as* JERRY *enters* L.I. MAY *and* JERRY *stand looking at each other.)* Hello, Jerry! Why—here's Jerry now, May.

JERRY. May, you've got to listen to me. You were right. I knew you were right the minute I walked off that set And I went straight up to Glogauer and told him so.

GEORGE. I told her, Jerry. I told her all about it.

JERRY. And so the answer is—here I am.

GEORGE. Here he is, May. We're all together again.

JERRY. Are we together, May? What about it, May? Are we together?

MAY. What the hell do you mean by leaving George alone here?

JERRY. Well, I wasn't going to stay here without you.

MAY. Then why didn't you come after me?

JERRY. I did!

MAY. All right, then.

GEORGE. Yes, sir, we're all together again. *(Suddenly* MAY *turns away from them—averts her face.)*

JERRY. What is it, kid—what's the matter?

GEORGE. Why, May!

MAY. *(Coming out of it)* I'm all right, gentlemen. Let a lady have her moment, for God's sake. It's just that we're together again, I guess. It's seemed so long.

JERRY. May, I can't ever forgive myself——

MAY. Don't, Jerry—you make me feel like a second-act climax. Well, from now on it's the Army with Banners, no matter what happens! George is the biggest man in Hollywood and we're riding the high wave!

GEORGE. No, we aren't, May.

MAY. What?

GEORGE. Mr. Glogauer is awful mad. I bought two thousand aeroplanes.

JERRY. You did what?

GEORGE. I bought two thousand aeroplanes.

MAY. What for?

GEORGE. I don't know. The man must have been a salesman.

MAY. Let me get this straight—— You bought two thousand aeroplanes?

GEORGE. That's right.

MAY. For Mr. Glogauer?

GEORGE. *(Nods)* I got one free.

JERRY. What! In God's name, George, what did you do it for?

GEORGE. Can't we do something with them? There ought to be some way to use two thousand aeroplanes!

MAY. Sure—make applesauce!

JERRY. Well, you can't lick that! It's all over but

the shouting, May. For God's sake, George, how could you do such a thing?

MAY. Well, there you are, Jerry, and what are you going to do about it?

GEORGE. Well, if somebody offered *you* an aero-plane——

GLOGAUER. *(Enters L.2, followed by* SUSAN *and* CROWD *of others)* Well, Doctor, we have done it again! Isn't it wonderful?

SUSAN. George!

GEORGE. Huh?

GLOGAUER. We have done it again! What a man you are, Doctor—what a man you are!

JERRY. What is this?

GLOGAUER. Miss Daniels! Mr. Hyland! Did you hear what the Doctor did? He went out and bought two thousand aeroplanes! Wasn't that wonderful?

MAY. *(Trying to get her bearings)* Wonderful!

JERRY. Wonderful!

GLOGAUER. The trend is changing, Miss Daniels— they just been telephoning me! Everybody wants to make aeroplane pictures, but they can't make 'em because the Doctor bought up all the aeroplanes! Every company is phoning me—offering me any amount!

GEORGE. Yes, I thought they would.

SUSAN. Isn't it wonderful?

GLOGAUER. So, Doctor, you saw the trend coming! You saw the trend!

MAY. Saw it? He *is* the trend.

JERRY. You don't realize the kind of man you've got here!

GLOGAUER. Yes, I do! Doctor—this is the way you work—always you make believe you are doing the wrong thing—and *then!* Doctor, I bow to you!

SUSAN. Oh, George!

MAY. George, you don't need us. You just go ahead and be yourself.

GEORGE. Mr. Glogauer, there's something we've got to take up.   *(WARN Curtain.)*

GLOGAUER. *(Anxiously)* What?

GEORGE. *(Pointing to open door* L.2, *through which* GLOGAUER *has just entered, and picture, which is not illuminated. Indignantly)* One of my pictures doesn't light up!

GLOGAUER. *(Greatly upset)* What! Meterstein! Weisskopf! (METERSTEIN *and* WEISSKOPF *say, "Yes, sir" and hurry off* L.2, *closing door behind them.)* Doctor, you're not angry! Tell me you're not angry!

MISS LEIGHTON. *(Entering* L.1) Mr. Glogauer—

GLOGAUER. Yes—?

MISS LEIGHTON. Do you know the studio's being torn down?

GLOGAUER. What?

MISS LEIGHTON. There're a lot of workmen downstairs. They have orders to tear down the studio!

GLOGAUER. Tear down the studio!

MISS LEIGHTON. Yes, sir!

GLOGAUER. *(Looks slowly to* GEORGE *to see if he is the man who gave the order; takes three steps toward him.* GEORGE, *scared at the entrance of* MISS LEIGHTON, *wears a broad grin of perfect confidence.* GLOGAUER *turns back to* MISS LEIGHTON*)* Tell 'em to go ahead! Tell 'em to go ahead! I don't know what it is. *(The CURTAIN starts to fall.* METERSTEIN *and* WEISSKOPF *enter* L.2, *having fixed the picture, which now lights.)*

METERSTEIN. O. K. now, Mr. Glogauer.

GLOGAUER. *(Without having stopped)* —but it'll turn out all right.

GEORGE. *(Seeing the picture light)* That's better! *(There is a GENERAL CONVERSATION and turmoil, with* EVERYONE *talking at once.)*

GEORGE. We're putting up a bigger one, Mr. Glogauer.

JERRY. Say, that's a good idea!

GLOGAUER. Wonderful! There's another trend coming, eh, Doctor?

GEORGE. Sure, sure!

SUSAN. Isn't he wonderful, May?

MISS LEIGHTON. *(At phone)* Construction Department, please——

THE CURTAIN IS DOWN

CURTAIN CALLS

ACT I

(From Left to Right)
1. FLORABEL, PHYLLIS, GEORGE, MAY, SUSAN, GLO-
   GAUER, JERRY, HELEN.

ACT II

(From Left to Right)
1. COMPANY *at Curtain.*
2. VAIL, MISS LEIGHTON, KAMMERLING, MRS.
   WALKER, HELEN, GEORGE, SUSAN, GLOGAUER,
   MAY, JERRY, FLORABEL, PHYLLIS.
   Down Left—Three SCENARIO WRITERS.
   *Up Left—*METERSTEIN, SCRIPT GIRL *and* CHAS-
   EN.
   *Up Right—*FLORABEL, PHYLLIS, *and* SECRE-
   TARY.
   *Down Right—*WEISSKOPF, 2 ELECTRICIANS *and*
   FLICK.
3. VAIL, LEIGHTON, HELEN, GEORGE, SUSAN, GLO-
   GAUER, MAY, JERRY.
4. GEORGE *and* MAY.
5. VAIL, HELEN, GEORGE, SUSAN, GLOGAUER,
   JERRY.

ACT III

(Left to Right)
1. LEIGHTON, GLOGAUER, SUSAN, GEORGE, MAY,
   JERRY.
2. GLOGAUER, SUSAN, GEORGE, MAY, JERRY.
3. GEORGE, MAY.
4. GLOGAUER, SUSAN, GEORGE, MAY, JERRY.

"ONCE IN A LIFETIME"

ELECTRICAL PLOT

ACT I—SCENE I (Night)

Center section foots, only.
Concert Border. (Low Trim.)
Strip. Right stage.
Bracket. Right stage. Lamp on table.

ACT I—SCENE II (Night)

All low trim.
Bracket lamps (2) in Pullman wall.
Concert border.
Foots. Center section only.
Buzzer in wall. Seat Right Center.

ACT I—SCENE III (Night)

Brackets. Up stage Right and Left Center. On
   backings.
Right and Left Center.
Baby spots. Off stage Left and Right.
Picture lamps. On ceiling drop. Off Left and Right
   stage.
X-Rays (Full up) (High trim).
Concerts (Full up) (High trim) Foots. (All sec-
   tions.)
Booth lights.

134

ACT II

Booth lights.
Concert and X-Ray borders on High trim.
Lights in Pilasters.
Telephone (practical, on desk).
Strips on each door (4).
Foots (all sections).

ACT III

Foots, all sections.
Concert Border (high trim).
X-Ray High trim.
Booth lights.
Three picture studio lamps.
Strips, off Left and Right stage.
Bell.

ACT III—SCENE II

Same as in First Pullman. (Act I, Scene II.)

ACT III—SCENE III

Same as in Act II, except for pictures of DR. LEWIS over doors that light when opened and closed.

"ONCE IN A LIFETIME"

PROPERTY PLOT

ACT I—SCENE I

Morris chair, down stage, Left Center.
Table, up stage adjoining Morris chair.
Indian nuts, copy of "Variety," ashtray (on table)
Bed. Right stage.
New York newspaper. (On bed.)
Chair, down stage Right.
Washbowl (not practical), up stage Left Center.
Towel rack, towels, over washbowl.
Rug, down stage, Right, at door.
Carpet under all.
Pack cigarettes used by MAY DANIELS.

ACT I—SCENE II

"Variety" on seat Right Center.
Book on seat Left Center.
Box Indian nuts seat Right Center.
New York newspaper, seat Left Center.
Pillow, carried on by PORTER.

ACT I—SCENE III

Chair down stage Left and Right.
Settees up stage Left Center and up stage Right
    Center, with ashtrays, etc.

Settees down stage Right and Left, raking toward
 Center.
Pillows, on settees.
Carpet under all.

ACT II

Chairs down stage Right and Left.
Two chairs flanking Pilasters up stage Right.
Two chairs flanking Pilasters up stage Center. Table
 Center.
Desk with modern lamp up stage Left.
Chair at desk up stage Left.
Card Index. Letters, papers, etc., on desk.
Cigarette holder, cigarettes, ashtray, etc., on desk.
Square buzzer, up stage Left.
Signs, Sign Holders. Silver coffee set. Papers for
 SECRETARY.

ACT III—SCENE I

Tripod Camera.
Rolling small camera.
Truck camera.
Copy of "Racing Form." Coin book. Newspaper.
Pews Left up stage. Raking off Left.
Bible. Candelabra (ecclesiastical). Small prayer
 book.
Two chairs. Down stage Center at beginning of
 scene.
Wedding-bell, hanging over altar.
Manuscript. Camp chair. Portable table, with phone.
Gold dinner set.
Ground cloth underneath.

ACT III—SCENE II

Bags underneath seat Left Center.

Newspapers (Los Angeles) (Two).
Book (seat Left Center).
Bags (2), carried on by PORTER.
Pillow (carried on by PORTER).
Telegram (carried on by PORTER).

ACT III—SCENE III

Silver box of Indian nuts.
Three manuscripts.

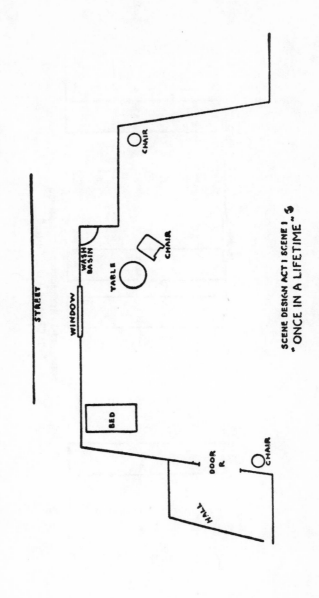

SCENE DESIGN ACT I SCENE I
"ONCE IN A LIFETIME"

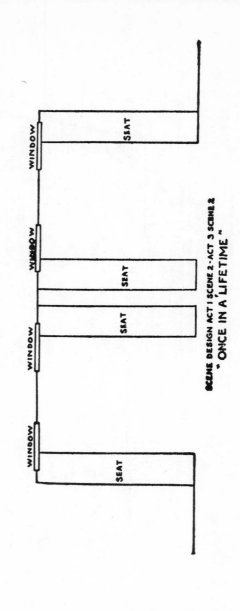

SCENE DESIGN ACT I SCENE 2 - ACT 3 SCENE 2
" ONCE IN A LIFETIME "

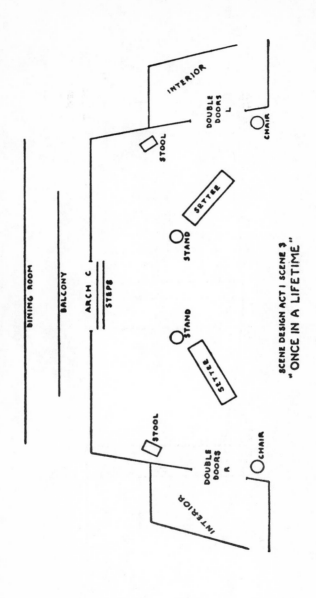

SCENE DESIGN ACT I SCENE 3
"ONCE IN A LIFETIME"

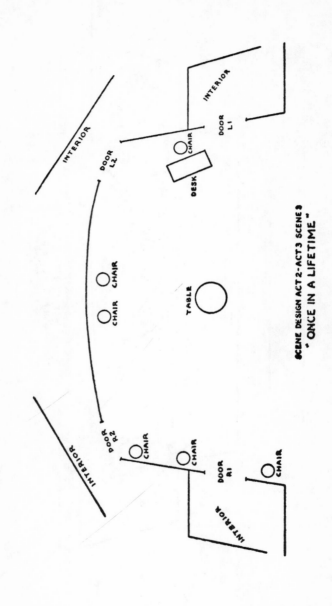

SCENE DESIGN ACT 2-ACT 3 SCENE 3
" ONCE IN A LIFETIME "

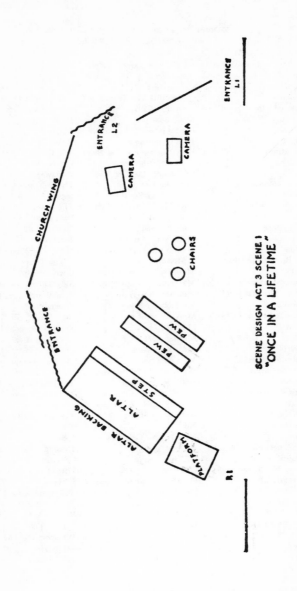

SCENE DESIGN ACT 3 SCENE 1
"ONCE IN A LIFETIME"

Popular Musical Productions Controlled by
SAMUEL FRENCH, INC.

Allison Wonderland
And I Ain't Finished Yet
Angel
Anne of Green Gables
Ballroom
The Best Little Whorehouse
  in Texas
By Strouse
Chicago
A Christmas Carol
Club, The
Cole
Comin' Uptown
Contrast
Cowardy Custard
Curley McDimple
Dames At Sea
Desert Song
Diamond Studs
Don't Bother Me I Can't
  Cope
Dracula Spectacular
Dracula: The *Musical*?
Drunkard
El Grande de Coca-Cola
Fashion
Festival
The First
First Impressions
Frank Merriwell
Golden Boy
Golden Rainbow
Goldilocks
Grand Tour
Grass Harp
Grease
Great American Backstage
  Musical
Growing Up Naked
The Haggadah
Happy End
Happy New Year
Heidi
Henry, Sweet Henry
H.M.S. Pinafore
Hijinks!
History of the American
  Film
Hot Grog
How Now, Dow Jones

I Love My Wife
I'll Die If I Can't Live
  Forever
I'm Getting My Act
  Together and Taking It
  on the Road
Ionescopade
It's So Nice To Be Civilized
Johnny Johnson
Kurt Vonnegut's God Bless
  You Mr. Rosewater
Last Sweet Days of Isaac
Lend An Ear
Little Mary Sunshine
Lock Up Your Daughters
Lovely Ladies, Kind
  Gentlemen
Mack and Mabel
Man With A Load of
  Mischief
March of The Falsettos
Marvelous Misadventures
  of Sherlock Holmes
Me Nobody Knows
Merry Widow
Mikado, The
Mother Earth
Musical Chairs
My Old Friends
My Son, The Astronaut
1940s Radio Hour
Noah's Animals
Nobody Loves A Dragon
Nobody's Earnest
Now!
Now Is The Time For All
  Good Men
Of Thee I Sing
Oh, Brother!
On The Twentieth Century
Operetta
Orpheus In The
  Underworld
Over Here
Peter Pan
Petticoat Lane
Piaf
Piano Bar
The Picture of Dorian Gray
Pirates of Penzance

Plain and Fancy
Pretzels
Prodigal Sister
"Progress May Have Been
  All Right Once"
Promenade
Purlie
Raisin
Robert and Elizabeth
The Rocky Horror Show
Rothschilds
Runaways
The Saloonkeeper's Daughter
Secret Life of Walter Mitty
The Seven
Seventeen
70, Girls, 70
Seesaw
Show Me Where The Good
  Times Are
Shenandoah
Slow Down, Sweet Chariot
Something's Afoot
Spokesong
Star Treatment
Street Dreams: The Inner
  City Musical
Strider
Student Gypsy
Sugar Babies
Ten Nights In A Barroom
They're Playing Our Song
Tom Sawyer
Trixie True, Teen Detective
Turkey in the Straw
2 by 5
Unsung Cole (And Classics
  Too)
Utter Glory of Morrissey
  Hall
Vagabond King
What A Spot!
What's A Nice Country
  Like You . . .
Whispers On The Wind
White Horse Inn
Wiz, The
Woman Overboard
You Never Know
Zorba